The Everyday Brother

Rommey Stepney Jr.

Bloomington, IN  Milton Keynes, UK

AuthorHouse™
1663 Liberty Drive, Suite 200
Bloomington, IN 47403
www.authorhouse.com
Phone: 1-800-839-8640

AuthorHouse™ UK Ltd.
500 Avebury Boulevard
Central Milton Keynes, MK9 2BE
www.authorhouse.co.uk
Phone: 08001974150

This book is a work of non-fiction. Unless otherwise noted, the author and the publisher make no explicit guarantees as to the accuracy of the information contained in this book and in some cases, names of people and places have been altered to protect their privacy.

© 2006 Rommey Stepney Jr.. All rights reserved.

No part of this book may be reproduced, stored in a retrieval system, or transmitted by any means without the written permission of the author.

First published by AuthorHouse 6/6/2006

ISBN: 1-4259-3523-0 (sc)

Library of Congress Control Number: 2006903717

Printed in the United States of America
Bloomington, Indiana

This book is printed on acid-free paper.

Acknowledgments

To God, the creator of life and love. Thank you Jesus, who died for my sins. Thank you for putting love and determination in me, to keep going on with life.

In loving memory of the grandparents that I knew: Vernon and Eva Stepney.

Granny, I still feel your love. Grandpa, I can still smell your corncob pipe you loved so much.

To Rommel and Imani, my beautiful children, I love and live for you, I'm with you always.

To Uncle Bug (Hubert Brown, Jr.), Uncle Bob Stepney, Uncle Roland Stepney, and Uncle PeeWee (Willie Stepney).

To my mother and father, you did the best you knew how.

To Lori, you stood and faced me when I felt the world turned it's back on me. Love infinity.

To you the reader, thank you, I love you.

Contents

911 1
The Move 9
Who's This? 23
A Different World 41
High School Low School 69
Decisions- Decisions 85
The Struggle To Turn 103
The System 113
The Breaking Point 129
The Great Pretenders 151
The Quest For Love 165

The Every Day Brother
911

Before the World Trade Center bombings that temporarily destroyed part of New York, there was me, Rommey Stepney Jr. born September 11, 1969 the seed of Rommey Sr. and Linda Faye Brown Stepney, both who are from West Virginia; mommy from Paceton and daddy from Thorpe. But as for me, I was born in Columbus, Ohio where daddy came in 1965. A poor ole country boy a long way from home, thought he'd leave the country hills to get a taste of the city life. As for mommy, she was still there waiting to finish her senior year at Gary High School class of 1966. I figure it had to be a difficult time for her because it was the first year of integration in West Virginia and most importantly, she was pregnant with her first child. Lashone.

The good thing about this though, was that daddy was going back to get mommy and marry her, but first he wanted her to finish school and most importantly she wanted that as well, and then they would be a family and move on. It's something how you plan to take one road in life, but then life throws you a curve ball and then you have to make other plans. I'm assuming this would be a big adjustment for the ex-football and track star, and an even bigger one for the ex-cheerleader and homecoming queen. But, it seems like a plan though right? I mean daddy going back to get mommy and all, going to the city to plan a better life for his young sweetie and newborn baby, and starting the young family life. To most of us, that sounds nice. Yeah, okay.

But before I go there, let me tell you where they came from. Daddy was born to Vernon and Eva Stepney, two people who believed in family and togetherness he also had three brothers; Roosevelt (Bobby), Roland, and Willie (Peewee) and one sister Florida Mae who passed away in 1959. Daddy's' nick- name was Curley, which later became Sunny when he moved to the city.

Mommy, who was born to Hubert and Wanda Brown, had four sisters and one brother; Marilyn, Wannetta, Mary, Dorothy, and brother Hubert Jr. Even though she had a semi- large family, her mother decided to leave her family behind to start her life over with a new man and move to White Plains, New York. This took place while they were young and unaware why their mother would leave them only to be raised by a part-time father and two aunts, Lula and Cula. I can't imagine how it feels to be raised without your mother, but I'm sure it was a big adjustment for someone to be without the woman who's womb you came out of, to nurture and support you to adulthood. On the flip side, what do you feel or don't feel to leave all six of the children who you carried in your body for nine months plus labor. In mathematic terms 54 months and several hours of labor, but again on the flip side she could've been thinking from mechanics terms, (parts plus labor.)

After graduation and marriage, my parents brought my sister into the world. Lashone was born in West Virginia in 1967. After commuting back and forth to Columbus, Ohio and West Virginia for two years, my family decided to settle in Columbus where I was born. We lived on the east side of Columbus where society classified it as The Hood. Maybe that was due to the pimps, prostitutes, bars, bootlegs, violence, and most of all, black people. In the hood, we lived in a large house that was broken down into 3 units, all one-room studios with a small kitchen and bathroom. We lived on the top level, which in the hood was known as the high-rise level. To my recollection, our ghetto high rise level was equipped with one large bed for my parents, a bed each for me and my sister, one couch, one small black & white television, a used coffee table, a kitchen table with one chair, and the bathroom, which was large enough for one adult to wash his or her butt with using minimal elbow room. But because my mother was a big fan of neatness, to my small frame, this looked like an immaculate one-floor castle. In this unit we called home, I was well protected, fed and clothed to the best of my mothers ability, and on occasions, I was allowed to go outside and play in the front yard under my mothers supervision from the top floor window.

As a child, all you see is play time and everything in motion not realizing the issues and responsibilities that a mother or father may have. But in my case a mother, but a father who was around. I guess as a child, seeing your parents together from time to time means everything is okay, and through my young innocent eyes, all is well and life is good. But to my surprise, moms was walking the line alone, and that line was a thin line between love, hate, and poverty. I wrote a song about it, you wanna hear it? Here it goes.

Sunny had already fallen victim to the city streets, and his presence started to fade. Maybe it was because there was a little more excitement; the stores, people, streets, jobs, and most of all, bars and prostitutes. These things seemed to absorb his mind and his time, and soon it would take control of his body, then it had his life.

Mommy, on the flip side was the opposite. She was focused on caring for her children and trying to get things together by working small jobs. She made very few friends, and the ones that she had were very good to her. They did things for her like take us to the store, job- hunting, and even down to the local welfare department. When there was no one around, she still made it happen. We walked. We walked to the laundry mat, yard sales, the community center, and to the store. Sometimes if she had enough change, we would get a ride from the ride hustlers for 50 cent or a dollar. But as you can guess, we walked most of the time.

During this time as a toddler, you're just in the world going along with whatever happens during the day that mom has to accomplish. And because my small body and mind was so full of curiosity, I had no clue what it was like to be responsible for small children and doing whatever it takes to stay on the right path for the sake of your seeds.

Shortly after, my young body was starting to take form and after a few butt whippings, I was starting to have a memory and notice right from wrong. But, also what I noticed was my father was missing in action for a day or two. Then when I saw him he would give my mom some butt whippings. But my young mind was asking "What did mommy do wrong?" "Did mommy break something around the house that I didn't know about? But there was also something that I noticed about Daddy, he seemed very different. His eyes were red, he seemed sluggish, and he seemed very, very mad. Little did I know my dad was a drinker. It seems that after some time in the city, my dad had already fell victim to the city life. For him and my mother it was much different than the country hills and coalmines of West Virginia, they also had a different frame of mind. Mom wanted to succeed, Dad wanted to have a good time. It seems for this poor old country boy a long way from home, his mind was slowly starting to change, from the family man he wanted to be, to the man who enjoyed the taste of the night life, fast times, and women.

During these times, my dads' presence became more and more distant. And during this time, there was no quality time; only brief visits with a little fighting involved. I can recall how nervous I would be when the fights would occur. It seemed like they were giants, with all the furniture tumbling, cursing, and sounds of flesh being battered. It seemed as though my mom was a mother lion protecting her young from the big giant bear. Soon my thoughts were "I'm mad at my Daddy and I'm going to beat him up when I get bigger!"

Through it all, my mother still tried to make it happen. We continued to walk to the store to get a little groceries, go to the laundry mat, to the local community center where we would play, to yard sales, and soon we would begin walking to church. Sometimes we would get a ride from the ride hustlers, or from my dad. But when he would come to pick us up, the cars were either borrowed or stolen. I think. After months of seeing the same thing, I continued to grow and have more of a memory. The good times spent with my mother, playing with neighborhood friends, long walks to any and every where, and those times I would see my dad off and on. They started with friendly hellos then sometimes violent goodbyes. Soon the pain would grow on my mothers face.

As a young kid, you have a lot of questions and sometimes you just don't get the answers. Not knowing that mom has so much on her mind to where she doesn't have the answers or just plain don't feel like talking. She's probably thinking about our next meal, the last fight, the next bill, or another sleepless night. Or she may have even been thinking about the right job, or even the next yard sale. Most of all, I think she may have been thinking where's my husband? Is he going to help? Don't you realize the fact that we need you? Why did you begin to break our marital agreement? Either way, I'm sure these were questions going through her mind and all the reason for a struggle to commence.

As the years go on, to my young eyes there was no noticeable improvement. I still recall not seeing my father often, but when I did, the time was still short and not much interaction. Sometimes I would hear him come in late and see his tall thin frame in the shadows moving up and down on my mom. Even though there was pain, maybe mom felt she still had a physical commitment to him as well. There was no resistance, only cooperation to avoid any more drama.

Along with all the other issues, I begin to take things real personal. I begin to notice that some of my toys my mother struggled to buy me were missing. One in particular my first new toy gun. With this gun, I would pretend to be a good cop slaying all the bad people in the world. Bank-robbers, thieves, murderers, and abusers. Come to find out, daddy was taking my gun on a daily basis. What was he using my gun for? Was it for robbery or intimidation? Either way, it was fake and it was just plain wrong. Even though I was scared of my dad, I mustered up the courage to ask "Daddy do you have my gun?" He said, "No I don't have your damn gun!" Then later, on his way out the door, I saw him take my toy gun from the couch cushion and place it in his pocket. I looked at him with hurt and disappointment while he looked at me like I dare you to say something. My mother watched like an innocent bystander. Soon my young heart encountered two new emotions, bitterness and rage.

Soon after my emotions started to grow, I began to identify with my mothers a little more and began to notice that her face looked different. She had puffiness around her eyes, which today we call bags. I saw the hurt and frustration. She was tired and ready for a change for the better. At first it seemed like just another day, but today was different. I could almost smell the frustration in the air. Change was coming.

The next day, I saw daddy and he had trouble in his eyes. But today mommy wasn't having it. Words exchanged and then the war began. Today the war was different because my mother fought back with a new strength. I always new she was strong, but today she seemed stronger than the ex football and track star. I remember earlier when my mom placed the largest butcher knife she had on the table almost in perfect plot and position. As my sister and I were spectators in fear we noticed my mom take her final blow to the face. My dad punched her in perfect position to grab the knife, when she got the knife she stabbed him with so much force it sounded like she was tearing into a fresh Georgia watermelon. Landing one inch from his heart, he knew he was defeated. He ran out of the apartment like an unsuccessful murderer to the local hospital for treatment. Even to this day, I can't stand the sound of someone slicing a watermelon.

Later that night, daddy returned to the house. I don't know what was exchanged as far as words, but what I do know was that she prepared a meal for him and he sat and ate peacefully watching the small black and white TV with a half cocked smile as if to say "No matter what happens I run this."

In my young developing mind, I began to ask myself "Is it okay to have such a violent encounter and then come home and interact with your family like nothing ever happened and never apologize to your kids for taking them through this?" At that point I had made up my mind that whatever I do to someone it should be, or better be accepted. Soon after, I began to feel numb at such a young age, and it got to a point where I didn't care if I had fun or saw violence. All I knew was I just wanted to make it to see life as an adult. Should I feel this way at nearly 5 years old? Well I did.

The Move

"Mommy where are we going? Mom. Mom." "What!" "I said where we going?" "We're moving." Before I knew it we were packing up our belongings preparing to move to another location. Even though I wasn't aware of it, I'm sure my mother had planned it for a while. I just had two questions in my mind: Were we moving up in the world, or were we moving to get away from my dad?

With the help of my uncle and his friend, we were packed up in a U-haul trailer and hooked to his car in no time. I rode in the back of the trailer stuffed behind some pillows for security. I thought the ride was fun, but the same old question arose in my mind. Where was my daddy? Was he even included in this move? And did he know we were moving?

While I was deep in thought, we had already arrived to our new home, which was only five minutes away from our last spot. Already one of my questions I had was answered. We weren't moving up in the world, we were just moving. On the outside, our new spot looked like two houses joined together made out of brick and wood. These two houses had a name that I would later be informed of, and that would be a Duplex or a Double. As I looked down the street, I noticed a lot of kids playing which meant one thing. I would soon have new friends. As I made eye contact with them, I grabbed a pillow to let them know I was the new kid on the block. As my eyes were satisfied on the outside, I was anxious to see what was on the inside. I ran to the porch to accompany my mom like I was her own personal bodyguard. As she opened the door, the living room seemed to be very large to my small frame. During the tour, I noticed everything was trimmed in dusty wood, but I knew that wouldn't last long once mommy put her cleaning skills to use. It was a lot of ground to cover, the first floor, second floor, attic, and basement. It was a major difference from our one room apartment with bathroom and kitchen.

During the tour, mommy waited to make our new rooms our last stop. My sister and I felt like it was Christmas waiting to see our private domains. First we saw mommy's room, which was large with chipped paint and mold. Then there was my sister's room, which was also a decent size with the same paint and mold. Then there was my room with the same chipped paint and mold. But one thing was different; I also had a kitchen sink and cabinets in my room. "Mommy" "What." " Why does my room look like a kitchen?" " Because you're the youngest." "And what does that mean?" It was then explained to me that our new home used to be two apartments. It then became self-explanatory we operate and receive things by age seniority. Before I knew it, my uncle, his friend, and my mom had our belongings in the house and ready to arrange. But now that we had more space, it seemed the house was still halfway empty. It took my young mind a minute to realize that.

"Mom, where's daddy?" "I don't know." It seemed that my dad was still semi in the picture like he'd always been, but I don't think mommy had it in the cards for him as far as the future was concerned. It was just something I felt in my young gut. Something became different about the times I saw my dad. It was like he was not in control of his body. And since he was no longer in control, he was not allowed to spend the night. The visits seemed to last only a few minutes and my mom was very distant and anxious for him to leave. With these visits, I noticed my daddy would sometimes cry and tell my sister and I that he loved us.

The Everyday Brother

This was something I had to get used to because all I could remember was the fighting at 1219 Bryden Rd. That was the old address. And now to this day every house is still there but that one.

I wouldn't dare ask anymore questions because I knew my mother didn't want to talk about it and when I saw my dad, I knew he didn't have any answers for me. So I did what anyone would do, I would keep my questions and feelings to myself, or keep them bottled up. That would soon be dangerous, for a five-year-old boy. My young mission now would be to adjust to my new environment and to move on without question. I don't know what my sister's mission was, but I could soon tell that my mother's mission was to care for her children and to be rid of my father.

After being somewhat adjusted, I would go outside to somewhat mingle with the neighborhood children. After mingling and getting to know them better, I noticed they were just like me, they had regular clothes mostly hand-me-downs or second hand, and they were just kids living to play and be happy. It seemed like after the move, time went so fast. Before I knew it, it was time to start school. My sister was already in school, so I was used to the walking. She went to a local catholic school on the east side of town. She always seemed happy to be going there, and mommy was happy for her. In my young mind, it seemed my mom was really trying to put it together, and continue to move forward, but there would still be many setbacks to come.

Today was my first day of kindergarten, and I was excited. I felt the long getaway from home and drama was much needed. I thought I looked good too. I had on a white turtleneck with a green & white-checkered sweater vest over top, some bell-bottomed jeans, and some earth shoes on my small feet. I was ready for this new chapter in my life. The walk to school seemed very long, probably because we had to take my sister first. I went to Douglas Elementary School, which was on the east side of Columbus. It was cool though because it was just a few side streets away from home and all the neighborhood kids went there. When we arrived, the school seemed huge to my small frame. A ton of kids were already there, playing and mingling with each other with a happiness, that I never seen. And a lot of these kids had on brand new clothes! Wow! Not that I didn't receive new clothes, but my mom had already mastered the used store trade. She could hit three stores or rummage sales in and hour and have combinations out of this world! Trust and believe I had some mean suits.

After plowing through the happy more experienced kids, mommy picked up instructions on how to get to the kindergarten class. When we arrived, the class seemed warm and homely. I was introduced to my teacher, Mrs. Bowls, who was very beautiful. She had that Joan Cleaver feel about her and the perfume she wore was comforting to my nose. I knew I would like this class with her as my teacher.

As I walked further into the classroom, I noticed a lot of other kids with their parents. The class was evenly mixed with both black and white students. Also, I noticed that a lot of the kids were crying and begging their parents not to leave them. This was mostly the white students, but there were a few spoiled blacks as well. But the rest of us were ready for this new adventure, we were ready to meet new people and be away from home. It was easy to see we were the inner city kids.

But, for the most part, kindergarten was fun and as time went on, all of us kindergartners became acquainted with each other and we enjoyed our ABC's and coloring projects together as one. And every once in a while, I would get a chance to cop a feel on Mrs. Bowls. I was a young nasty.

But, after a full day of kindergarten, it was time to go home. Because of the all day class, I had grown to miss my mom on a daily basis, and couldn't wait to see her. Just to hold her hand walking down the street and telling her about my day was comforting to me. It kept my mind off of the drama in the past and feelings of fear.

The walk home was always nice because I got to mingle with the after school crowd of different ages and personalities. From the petite little girls to the kids that looked like ghetto pig-pins, we all formed a neighborhood bond after school. I always admired the older kids because they walked home by themselves. I couldn't wait to get a little older.

When we got home, it was time for an after school snack and possibly some play time. I had gotten well acquainted with my neighborhood friends and they would make frequent visits to my house. But because my mom was cautious, they were only allowed on the porch, not in the house! Sometimes I would be allowed in the street, but only in front of the house and watch for cars.

It seemed that all of the other kids had so many other privileges. Like they didn't have to be in front of the house, they could go to the store by themselves, allow people in their houses, and a list of other things that I wasn't allowed to do. But I knew in time, I would be allowed those privileges. But for now, I was happy for all of the other kids who had so much space.

After the long day, it was time to eat. Mommy made it a point to make sure we had some kind of food in our stomachs. Like most single black mothers, the meals would change depending the time of year and month. From Ham and Turkey during the holidays, Oh yeah, Chitterlings too, to Chicken, Pork Chops, Beef Stew, Chicken and Dumplings, all the way down to Bologna and Beans. Today was a Beans and Hot Dog day. I used to cut my hotdogs up and put them in the beans. That was what I call Ghetto Casserole.

To a young boy who hasn't seen much but the East Side of town, this was the life and it was much appreciated. I always admired the busyness in my mother and how she kept moving through her situation. As a child your mind isn't programmed or mature enough to consider your parents feelings, but looking back on things, the look in her eyes showed pain and disappointment. But guess what? She kept right on rolling.

After the meal, there was usually a knock on the door or a bang I should say. Guess who? Yeah you guessed right, it was Big Rommey. I knew things had really changed because he wasn't allowed in the house. My sister and I would wait in the background because we didn't know if there would be drama. After my mother would find out that it was my dad, I would study her face to see her reaction. She would say: "Aw Naw it's your Daddy" and prepare for any possible war. After telling him several times he couldn't come in, and threatened to call the police if he tried to, we were allowed to come out on the porch and visit with him for a few minutes. I became afraid of my dad because of the things I saw him do to my mother with such heartless fury. But I also had missed him very much and just wanted to talk to him, and know that he was okay. I know that he wanted the same for my sister and I, that's why he came. I could tell he missed my mother too, but she wasn't having it, because he was out of control and he wasn't about the family. I felt she missed him too and still loved him by the look in her eyes. Thing is, one eye said love, and the other eye said, "You're no good you're no good you're no good, baby you're no good." Remember the song? But through all the feelings, we welcomed his short drunken visits. And believe me he was smashed with a spare bottle in his back pocket for the road. Nervously, we would listen to what he had to say without much response and I hoped like hell my mommy wouldn't say anything smart while observing from the screen door because if she did, it might be some drama.

Soon the visit would have to end and he would grace us with a drunken hug with the smell of sour liquor and the sting from his stubbly beard and head back into the streets for more trouble. But before he left he would have to get rid of his dinner to make more room for the bottle in his back pocket. He would stick two fingers down his throat and throw up his dinner, which consisted of two chilly dogs from JP's restaurant on Main St. JP's was off the hook! How dare throw that up! But the liquor in his stomach was more important. The visit wasn't a visit if that didn't take place. This routine went on for a while, but most of all I loved school, my friends, and where I lived. I was beginning to take form.

During my elementary period, things seemed to settle with me except the fact that I could never get used to not spending any quality time with my dad. And again, when I saw him he was always drunk and on edge. But that would never take my mother off course from raising her kids. While at school, even though I was having a good time and enjoying time away, I couldn't help worrying about my mother and would she be safe from the monster. Would he show up even though my sister and me weren't there? What state of mind would he be in? But when the bell rang, my young mind would be put at ease because mommy would be there faithfully to pick me up. I really adored my mother in a special way. She always looked nice and her hair was always combed. At this time it was a short Afro. She began to smile, which I hadn't seen in a while. That told me she would continue to do the things she needed to do to care for herself and her children. Regardless of what daddy was doing. Mom had a program to run and she was running it, or walking it I should say. We continued living the best we could which included the walks to the store, the laundry mat, yard sales, and to church. I continued to observe my mother closely and protect her with my own mind.

As a youth, you never realize why you have to do things that don't pertain to cartoons and playing. Sometimes I would ask in silence why do we have to walk everywhere or why doesn't mom have a car like everyone else or why can't I just stay at home while mom does all these things. In a very unique way as children we are all selfish, and total appreciation comes with age and experience. Our living went on and mommy continued to do the best she could by making sure we were housed, fed, clothed and educated. Time would begin to pick up and as we were making slow changes, it seemed like daddy was still the same.

Some of the changes included; more furniture in the house, a bigger black and white TV, advancement in school, and my mother was even working. That meant there was a possibility for newer clothes and shoes on a regular basis, more sweets to eat and most of all, I would get to walk to school by myself. Or maybe I should say with my sister and all of the other neighborhood kids, so that meant I wasn't totally independent. I felt they cramped my style. I had some nerve because I was the youngest.

Soon school was out for summer vacation, and I was glad. Even though I loved school, I was ready for fun. All day fun! My bubble was soon busted when I was informed my sister and I would be going to a babysitter for the summer while mommy worked. This was unexpected, but I had to except it.

The trip to the babysitter's house was a ten-minute walk from home. Yeah that's right, we're still getting that exercise, but it was cool. I didn't mind walking in the summer for short distances.

When we arrived at the babysitter's house, I could tell my mother searched really well for this one. The house was a well-groomed one, and on the porch waiting, was a beautiful woman in her mid fifties standing there anxious for us to arrive. Her name was Mrs. Floyd, and she seemed to be very polite and mannered. Inside the house the furniture was neat and everything was polished. Mrs. Floyd was not alone she had a husband who's name was Mr. Floyd.

Mrs. Floyd was well kept. I could tell back in her days she was fine. Just by looking at her skin tone, hair, and legs. Not only was she well kept her babysitting program was tight. We ate, played, watched TV, and took a nap everyday at the same time religiously. We also had good snacks. Ain't nothing like having a babysitter with fresh PB & J's and good snacks. Moms hit the jackpot! To add to that, Mrs. Floyd helped in teaching my sister and I respect and manners. She also would humor us by telling us a joke from time to time. Now a days, you're lucky to find a babysitter who's place isn't over crowded, not feeding or changing your kid, feeling your kid up in the corner, or just plain shaking your baby to death. You know: Baby Shaking Syndrome. And to add on top of that, Mr. Floyd was a very hard-working man with a serious face. Not that he was mean or anything, he was just about his business. I admired him because I saw him go to work everyday in his neatly pressed uniform ready to take on whatever comes his way. It was kind of funny, because at such a young age, I had a high respect for people who worked. Probably because I saw my mother working and doing what needed to be done just so we could have a place to lay our heads and eat. The Floyds were another example of that.

Even though I enjoyed being away at the babysitters, my mind would still wonder if my mom was okay, and was she safe from the monster. You know, Big Rome. I knew in my young heart he was still out there and he wasn't done with us yet. But at the end of the day, I would get the word from Mrs. Floyd that it's almost time for my mom to get off work so I would wait patiently hoping she would make it here in one piece. And to my surprise, she would come walking around the corner. I was always happy to see her. I guess grown folks would say I missed her.

After greeting us with a smile, and respectfully thanking Mrs. Floyd for caring for us, we would start our journey home. The short walk always made it nice which allowed me to have more free time to play during the long summer day. As a youth, you only experience being on one side of the fence and that's the receiving side. Only eat, play, eat, and play. We have not yet had the opportunity to get up and get yourself and the kids ready, go to the babysitter then catch the bus or walk to work, then work all day for someone who really didn't want to give you a job anyway, worry about your kids safety, get off work, catch the bus or walk back to the babysitters house to pick up your kids, then walk home. And I had the nerve to cop an attitude when mom would say: " Let your mother get some rest before y'all go outside to play."

Looking back on things, even though we didn't have much, I still enjoyed the life I had and made it fun. What else can you do as a child? A lot of us don't know what it is to have had and lost things like cars, furniture, other material things, especially money. All we know is the struggle of a single mother and being a child in the middle. Summer was still fun and through all of the playing, going back and forth to the babysitter, the store, yard sales, the laundry mat, and church, to me life was good and I began to observe my surroundings a little more. In my observation, I noticed my mother paid a lot of attention to my actions and what I did as far as my attitude and personality. It was almost like how has he been affected behind what has gone on so far in his life. I also noticed my father's visits became shorter and more drunken. But through that, I thought I was cool and full of comedy. My nickname was Little Man, which came from my uncle Peewee who was my father's youngest brother. He called me that because every time he saw me I had on a nice little suit and hat, looking just like a little man. So that's what mom stuck with. At a young age, I thought it was more mature than PooPoo or Mooky. I was a trip.

The way mom took care of me made people see me that way. That was powerful! I appreciated the acknowledgement of being Linda Faye's son Littleman. My neighborhood friends still called me Rommey, but inside I was a little man which I couldn't wait to become one.

Well, summer was almost over and right about now I was ready to move on move up in age and grade. All of the playing would have to slow down to get adjusted to the routine school schedule. When school started, it was another new experience. I remember some of the students from last year, and there were also new ones along with all of the other kids from the neighborhood. Because Douglas was now an Alternative School, the variety changed as far as kids coming from different backgrounds. From high class to low class, we were all there. That went for the teachers as well. They all loved us and they taught us well. I liked Douglas Elementary because the teachers wanted to see us improve and we had a boatload of fun! It also gave them a sense of accomplishment. From Field trips to animals and baking sweets, we did it all. In that time, I started paying more attention to the girls as well. Even though I loved school, and playing smear the queer at recess, the girls still caught my young eyes. One girl in particular, her name was Veronica. She became my sweetheart, which lasted most of my elementary years.

Veronica was a pretty young girl who was of the mixed complexion, smart, and had a great sense of humor. She came from what seemed to me a well-rounded family. To me that meant having both parents in the home. What I initially noticed was the silver caps in her mouth. You know the ones you get as a kid from the dentist to cover the cavities. She had two in the front looking like a high-tech vampire, and I had four altogether. That was enough to make my approach. After that, we became an elementary item.

It's funny how as a youth you think you got it going on because you have a little girlfriend and you call yourself claiming your territory when anyone tries to get next to your lady. What did we do? Challenge our competition to a race, or make sure we brought the pain when it came to smear the queer. I was an athlete early, so most of my challenges went unmet. And Veronica was mine for a while.

At a young age, we placed demands on our young black girls. As black boys we fell in the mode early of claiming something or someone that we had no rights to or worked for. "Will you be my girlfriend? If so, check yes or no." Before long, we inner city kids would learn that we don't own a damn thing! Other than becoming selfish at an early age, school was great and I enjoyed the interaction with the other kids that I shared part of my young life with. Even though we had different lives outside of school we had good relationships with one another, and for the most part, we couldn't tell the differences in each others lives because we were too busy being children.

After school, it was back home and to the fear of the fact that anything could happen at any given time when it came to my father. His visits were still short and drunken, and there was a distant fire in his eye. I wouldn't be happy until my memory of the past would fade, or if there was at least a sober visit. But most of all, I was already mad and bitter and knew how to hide it very well. There was no way in the world I would allow anyone to see the hurt and disappointment that I felt, especially at school.

For example, I can remember the time my mom allowed my dad to take me for a ride on the handlebars of a bike, suddenly my foot got caught in the spokes full pedal stride and damn near tore my foot off. I mean blood, bone and all and he left me down the street to walk home. But guess what, mom came to get me. That's when she officially became "mommy" instead of mom. But I couldn't walk for almost a month! I say this to say I wanted a memorable moment to happen with my father and it turned out to be a nightmare with no apology then or later. Things like that make a young boy bitter and later turn into a dangerous man. In my opinion, it's the innocence that allows us to give opportunity after opportunity even though we know that more than likely the end result will be disappointment.

Soon at such a young age, my disappointment became fury that burned so deep that I could only explain it now as an adult. My dreams of playing ball and going to ball games with him turned into nightmares of slicing his throat and beating him down when I became of age and decent size. News flash! Today I found out that a twelve- year old boy died this weekend in a car accident that was caused by a seventeen-year old girl. My dad thought I should know. But guess what? That twelve-year old boy was my brother, whom I never knew. Today is June 6, 2005. I'm 35 and he was 12. Do the math. Man Shh never stops! But anyway, I soon wanted to forget him because he brought nothing but pain to my young insides and that burn would soon become a back draft. I truly didn't want to burn anymore and the best thing I could do was to put a chill on my young heart. I don't know if any of you out there had feelings like I had at such a young age, but it can cause problems if not resolved somehow. Problems like anger, bitterness, and self- destruction. I wanted to forget about him so I could be a kid not just on the outside, but on the inside as well.

Soon his visits became that, just visits and there was no smile on my face only obeying the orders from my mom to just sit on the porch and talk to him for a minute. The only feelings I had were feelings of fear and that fear was for my mother hoping that there would never again be any violence against her. I just wanted him to fade away. For a lot of young blacks, when our family is broken, so are our hearts and lives and without proper acknowledgement of this, a broken heart can turn into a disease that can take over our entire being and transform us into something or someone we never dreamed of becoming. I just wanted dad out of my insides! Time continued to move on, and we lived like most single-parent families. Mom was doing what she could do, and I was living as a young boy in the low-class part of the city, and having a low-class life, and expressing low-class feelings.

Who's This?

One thing mom continued to do was take us to church. Faithfully every Sunday we would walk to church. Now mind you, mom did her best at turning me out as far as the mini- suits, so I knew I was sharp. But I wasn't too cool with walking near a mile in my little dress shoes. We attended Hopewell Baptist Church on the east side of the city. It was on Main St. where all of the action was. There were drugs, wine, prostitution, fighting, and stealing. But you know what? God plants his seeds everywhere! Hopewell was a small church with maybe 14 members max on a good Sunday. But I enjoyed it because it was positive. Yeah, I knew what positive was as a kid, so be cool. We did everything that the big churches do, have Easter and Christmas plays, church picnics, and three offerings a Sunday. Yeah, you know the Sunday School Offering, Tithes and Offering, and the Building Fund. I guess the building fund helped us to move down the street to another location. Sometimes you never see any results from the building fund at churches and you pay into it for a while.

As I continued to attend church, I noticed we had a few members join our small fellowship. There was one person in particular. He was a slim young man and very good looking. The thing about it, he acted like he looked good. He wore what the cool men wore at that time, which was a wide-collar silk shirt, skin-tight polyester bell-bottomed pants, 3-inch heel dress shoes, and a 5-inch afro to top it off. Now, that attire is only allowed at old-school parties.

I noticed this man because he and my mother were making eye contact, and it was different from any kind of church fellowship eye contact. You know sometimes as a child you notice a lot of things that you're not supposed to, but I dare not to ask any questions because so many of my questions had already went unanswered. To my curious findings, Mr. Cool was the brother of the pastor of the church who was from Louisiana, who called himself J. Which was his cool nickname I guess. He was another man from southern country who wanted to get a taste of Columbus Ohio. Because I was young, I wasn't filled in on a lot of the details. Meaning I was to stay out of grown folks business. I say that to say this: Mr. Cool was at my doorstep! Now I know we weren't having church at home so why was he here? Oh hell no! Mommy likes this dude and he's coming to spend time with her!

Now I don't know what was wrong with me, but I didn't like that. He was cool and all, but I ain't for mommy spending time with no man unless it's my daddy. And besides that, he would be taking time from me. It's time to show out!

As children coming from broken homes, we don't pay attention or even realize that our mothers have needs we just make childish assumptions that no matter what mom goes through, she's only to be with Bio dad. We overlook their tears, swollen eyes, and broken hearts.

But the selfish kid in me noticed the smile on both their faces, and that smile said they wanted a future. So I cut up, acted up, and guess what? I got my butt whipped right there in that very spot. Because you know black mothers back then didn't play that time out stuff, it was on anywhere in front of anybody. All of a sudden I wanted my daddy. I was a trip. Because I noticed looks a lot, through my tears I looked at him

The Everyday Brother

and to me, his look said, " Man I'm not trying to deal with nobody's kids." The look was a very strange look, that I never seen him display at church before, so I knew there were more strange looks to come. My wishes for my dad to arrive became stronger.

Not that I really wanted to see him, because the disappointment and bitterness had set in, but I wanted him to run some kind of interference. In modern terms it would be cock blocking or something like that. In modern math it would look like this: Interference + cock-blocking = hating. I wanted my dad to hate on him so bad I could smell, taste, and burp it!

But once again, daddy never came when I needed him. Even though it was for the wrong reasons, he didn't come through. Then my disappointment had offspring disappointments. But you best believe he would come though. My thoughts of my father never failed to breeze through my mind. Even though fear and hurt were there, I wanted him around. Was it more pronounced now that there was a possibility of another man trying to break down my mother's wall of abuse and disappointment? I wasn't sure. This is too much for a young boy to take. Now mind you, I thought he was cool, but it was about being cool without being around my mother. It was just something about that I couldn't and didn't want to accept. Do you know what I mean, or do you know somebody who knows what I mean?

When it was time to go to church, I looked at him differently now, and his title had changed from the cool guy to the cool dude who's trying to get with my mom! Even though I was looking at him out of the corner of my eye, he did something to warm the chill that I had. As our little choir was singing, he strides behind the piano and starts playing in tune with the singing. Man this dude had a jazzy play about him that I admired. And the smirk on his face was as if he was saying: " I got plenty of tricks up my sleeve young fella, so be cool." I admired his sarcastic smirk. It was like that sly smirk that the actor Leon had in the Five Heartbeats or Waiting To Exhale.

Later in the conversation, I heard that Mr. Cool played the piano by ear. After inquiring what that meant, it means he had not taken music lessons he just played the piano off of any sounds he heard. Since I didn't really have a man figure in my life, as a young boy I guess I was willing to accept anyone or anything that did something pleasing or interesting that filled me with excitement. Was that good? Well I wasn't quite sure but after witnessing that talent, I was ready to give him a shot.

Even though I was willing to give him a shot, something told me on the inside that daddy wasn't going to like that. Even though he didn't come around much and didn't care how his son was raised, I still had that feeling. Since he was already controlling and halfway intimidating, I knew he would have a problem with another man being around his ex-wife and kids. Men y'all know how we do it: life is supposed to end, and no one else can be with the mother of your children.

Mr. Cool continued to visit and I continued to admire him, but I knew time would soon come when my dad saw his face. Daddy also continued to visit, but I became more disappointed in him. He was still drunk and he would do things like hand me money and then five minutes later he would take it back and say he would give it to me later. Little did he know this disappoints a child and is stored in the memory for later use or abuse. Nothing could stop me from giving him opportunity to make me happy and I wanted this even more since there was someone else who had one foot in the door to my mother's heart. I had developed a great stamina and endurance for heartbreak and disappointment.

Soon the door would open for any male figure to come into my life with full force and as a child, all I could do was accept him without any strength to put up a fight. And that male figure was Mr. Cool. He was in with my mom, and now he was in with me.

When daddy found out about Mr. Cool, I didn't sense any heartbreak, only vengeance. I could tell by the look in his eye he had an attitude.

Like my mother was supposed to go on living her life without anyone to hold her, comfort her, and make her happy. Men you know how it is: all we're thinking about is the unhappy sight of another man between the legs of your ex. And that's all we're thinking about until we mature.

If Daddy had any chance of coming back in the past, now it was over. This was the first man I can recall my mom being with, and to me she was going to make it stick. I don't know if she was tired of being alone, or waiting on daddy to change his ways, but that was at an end. It was time to adjust to the relationship going further, or any drama that may take place. Remember I saw vengeance.

In that Mr. Cool was making more frequent visits, and I grew to like him even more. As children we notice so much and just like adults, we want peace and happiness. I no longer wanted to live in fear of what might happen from one day to the next. I wanted to smile like happy little boys should smile, not have a smile on one side and a frown on the other. Daddy hadn't given up on his family, and because the street had crucified him, he probably didn't know what had been taking place. As a matter of fact, he didn't know.

One day while daddy was in the house, and we got a visit from the church pastor and his wife. While he was upstairs, he overheard them making plans to meet up with the pastor's brother Mr. Cool. Daddy was so upset he ran them up out of there. This left me confused, one minute, daddy wasn't allowed in the house, and the next minute he was. Little did they realize, this kind of stuff leads to total confusion. To me confusion without communication can be deadly. So deadly, it can affect a child later in life. You'll see.

In that, there was a little drama between Daddy and Mr. Cool. I don't know if daddy felt he was losing his kids because he had already lost his ex-wife. And it became Mr. Cool keeping daddy out of the house instead of mommy. And before I knew it, the visits from Mr. Cool became all night stay-overs and sometimes he would even leave some clothes. You know what that means. If a brother starts leaving clothes, he's claiming the turf or trying to move in. Just like a dog pissing on his territory. Just like a dog. Did I like it? I wasn't sure. Maybe I liked it because that was what my mom wanted. I wasn't sure because I was confused remember?

And before I knew it Mr. Cool was up in the crib like a new college freshman moving into the dorms. It was no more come and go, no more spend the night and leave, it was waking up to the smell of a grown mans fart coming down the hallway.

To a degree, I didn't agree with this because something in me wanted my dad to be the one moving in. Even though he was a big disappointment, he was still my dad and as a child sometimes we think no matter what goes on or who gets hurt, dad should still be in the starting lineup.

Or maybe I didn't agree because I was no longer the latest addition to the family, and I saw how I wasn't getting the attention that I used to get. You know how we do it; we get salty when all the smiles from mommy don't pertain to us. Was this just the way I was feeling? Is this just part of being a boy? Hell I wasn't sure. And remember too much was already on my mind.

When the visits would occur from daddy, I could see in his eyes that the vengeance was no longer there, only hurt and sorrow. He knew Mr. Cool was the latest addition to 1139 Fair Ave and there was nothing he could do about it. He was at war with the streets and alcoholism and he was losing fast. He lost his wife, and felt he was losing his kids to another man. When an alcoholic has things like that on his brain, that's more reason to drink. And with every drunken visit there were tears to follow. I began to feel sorry for my dad.

Mr. Cool on the other hand, didn't too much care for him coming over. I don't know if it was because of the drama, drunkenness, or the insecurity of the fact of being the first man in mom's life. Men some of you know how we think; if it's over, it's over. And could care less if the ex saw his children or not. The act of being secure about your position in the household comes with maturity.

Speaking of maturity, Mr. Cool was some years younger than my mother, and it would soon start to show. He became a little more arrogant, and his stride had more of a limp to it. He stayed in the mirror and he took longer getting dressed than my mother did on Sunday. He believed in shining his shoes and his car the first thing in the morning on weekends. Not that it was a bad thing but there was just too much pride involved. You know how some people just go overboard?

Mommy on the other hand was enjoying her relationship not paying that any mind. I think she was just focused on having a man around. She rolled out the red carpet for him in ways that I wasn't able to understand. Not taking any time to talk to me about it, she jumped in with both feet rolling hard. As children, I think we deserve a little more communication about situations, so we're not just there to figure out things on our own.

I say that to say this; He got better treatment and I couldn't understand why. I would have to wait until he used the bathroom first, no matter how bad I had to pee. He got to wash up or take a bath first and he got pancakes and eggs while I ate cereal. And if I was still hungry, which I was, my mom told me to wait to see if Mr. Cool was going to finish all of his food. So I would wait at the edge of the table to see if he was going to complete his breakfast like a hungry little puppy. What the hell was going on!

What was going on was there was no equal balance between mommy's two children and her new man. Not that we were totally out of the picture, but we were pushed slightly to the side just so she could please her new man. I was a boy with a sharp mind and noticed a lot, and you can best believe I noticed it.

I'm sure Mr. Cool noticed it too, but he was too cute to even try to add to the balance it was about him and he enjoyed it. So much so it got to the point he would call me all the way down stairs to turn the television, or all the way upstairs to get him some toilet paper as he sat on the pot waiting and the closet was right next to the bathroom. Man I didn't want to smell his stuff!! Sorry for getting mad.

Even though these little things irritated me, I guess I still enjoyed having him around. I think maybe it was because I wanted to be cool like him when I got older. You know, sometimes as kids we just can't wait to get big, and sometimes we want to be like the grown folk that are around us. Whether good or bad, we end up inheriting some of their traits whether we want to or not.

Time flew and before I knew it, mommy and Mr. Cool were tying the knot. It was a small wedding in the house with the attendance of family and a couple of friends. And because children aren't allowed in grown folks business, it hit me from nowhere.

Daddy was still visiting, but the visits were few and far between. I could tell he was emotionally lost and more addicted to alcohol more than ever before. I began to become disgusted with him because not once did he value his family enough to fight for us. Mind you, Mr. Cool was cool, but dad was dad. If I had a choice in the matter I would fix dad myself and make it work. But I fantasized at an early age too.

Life as a young boy became rough for me because I couldn't understand why I thought about the things I thought about, but yet I was too young too talk about it. So once again I kept my feelings bottled up and tried to be a boy. I played with my neighborhood friends going through the motions of playing kickball, smear the queer, high-water-low-water with emotional things on my mind. I was able to juggle my feelings like a circus employee.

On the other side, mommy and Mr. Cool were doing their thing and I guess they were doing it well because mommy starts looking a little plump. At that time I wasn't thinking about happy or comfortable weight, I just knew she was picking up. And as the days went by, her mid-section went from cantaloupe, to volleyball, to watermelon. Mommy was pregnant!

I didn't know if I should say "Aw hell no" or "hell yes" because I didn't know where I would fit in. But since mommy was happy, I guess I would be too. But in reality I didn't really have a choice now did I?

So I said yes to my future brother or sister because looking at the size of my moms belly it was a done deal.

Mr. cool on the other hand became even more cool and cocky because now he had a permanent stamp on the situation and he had his own child coming into the world. This also meant mommy was starting all over again in the life of mothering. I didn't see room for me in this up and coming situation and not only that Mr. Cool needed a lot of attention. I would soon be just another kid that a mother had.

As time continued to go on, I continued to be happy for my mom because she was a happy expectant mother with a young husband who enjoyed working and looking good. She liked what was going on without any second glances at what I might be going through as a young boy. I felt it didn't matter so I mastered the game of fake smiles, and fake playing in the neighborhood with my friends. Even taking the time to rub her belly, and feeling the baby in her belly kick, as my rating of excitement was only 45 percent.

But at night, I would bite my lip because I still wanted my dad around and I was hurt from what I felt and saw in the past without getting any comfort. As I listened to them laugh and play, I wondered why that couldn't be my real daddy in there feeling like he's the man. I would bite my lip so hard sometimes it would bleed, and I would soon have visions of violence because there was no conversation of the man who planted the seed in my mother so I could have life. There was no me without any comfort or explanation.

Mommy used to give me attention, but to me that became a slight memory. I wouldn't say that I was totally ignored, but I became a job. I say that to say she made sure I was dressed and ate but there was no time for extra one on one. Don't get me wrong, I had plenty of fun but I craved an extra hug, an extra smile, or even an I love you from time to time.

As a child sometimes we are overlooked in the area emotion, heartache, and heartbreak. We need to be nurtured back to good inner health just as adults do. And to a degree, I felt moms was only thinking about herself and what she felt she needed mentally and physically. Without any regard to the inner feelings of her offspring, she went from one life to the next and left me in the middle. We are little human beings you know.

While captured in the web of childhood emotion, the next addition to the family was arriving into the world. It was early spring, and he was as bright as the sun he rode in on. I was happy for mom and dad and happy about the fact that I had a little brother. Oh yeah, by the way I was calling Mr. Cool dad since he was my new stepfather. But I would never let my real dad know for fear it might make him mad.

Little bro was a gorgeous young man with a smile and smooth skin like his father. I can tell dad was proud to have his first born a son. I became attached in a hurry because love for a new sibling is automatic no matter how you feel about other things. So I had to change my role from hurting little boy to big brother because some day he would look up to me. I was nine years old, but I felt like nineteen holding my little brother.

The Everyday Brother

I watched mommy change her mode also from hard-working woman to a complete housewife. At that time I didn't know about maternity leave or nothing like that, I just new she wasn't working. Dad was still working so I knew there was work in the household. I didn't know about income either, I just knew there was work.

I think mommy enjoyed being at home because that gave her time to focus on little bro and things around the house. It was summer again, so I got to experience new things like summer camp and free lunch programs. Free lunch was some thing that was held in the low- income neighborhoods for kids to come and eat cold-pack lunches for free. Man! the lines used to be down the street. And in those lines there were a lot of boys and girls who felt just like me.

This free lunch program was held by an organization called CMACAO, which stands for Columbus Metropolitan Area Community Action program. This program also helped families with other things too like heating assistance, and paying bills that low-income families, may have problems with. To a lot of black families CMACAO was truly a blessing. I know one thing those cold sub sandwiches, chocolate milks, and sugar cookies were the bomb! I used to ask the smaller kids: "You gonna eat your sugar cookie?" They used to look at me like I was crazy. Because just like me, they were still hungry too.

As a growing young boy, I developed an appetite that was out of this world. Like all other kids, the more we played and grew, the bigger our stomachs got. But in my household, just because my appetite grew with my body, my food portions didn't change. For breakfast it was one bowl of cereal, dinner no extras either, and a light snack. But guess what? Dad ate whenever he wanted to. I couldn't understand the unfairness in the household. Something else was going on. If there was work, why was I only allowed small portions? Did someone not care if my hunger was satisfied? I needed answers.

But I was thankful for the free lunches and the summer camps, because they were temporary relief. And because I kept my feelings to myself, I rode the wave of childhood bitterness, and uncertainty. It was like the untold feelings I had was turning into a powerful infection that was just spreading everyday. There's nothing like being mad and hungry.

Sometimes I would look forward to Fridays because it would be a little extra involved. When mom had it, we would make popcorn on the stove and watch the late night scary movies on TV. It was called Chiller, and man was I excited. Moms made some of the best popcorn on the stove. Remember that? And when you started shaking the pot and hear the flurry of popcorn, man it was on. Little things like that took away the pain for a while, and after that it was Saturday morning cartoons.

Saturdays were nice because it was an early morning marathon of cartoons. Bugs Bunny, School House Rock, Fat Albert, The Jackson Five, Super friends, Speed racer, and so much more. They brought laughter and imagination into my boyhood world that I could live with forever. I depended on these televised events to bring me joy that I couldn't receive in my real world. Then sometimes my joy would end early because my stepfather would come down and make me change the TV channel.

He was killing my spirit in many ways. Sometimes he would even humiliate me in front of my neighborhood friends. You see, because I was the fastest kid on my block and every one knew it. Sometimes I would even get challenges from kids from different neighborhoods and I would blow their doors off. Then sometimes after being victorious and getting props from the neighborhood, he would come out and challenge me. So we would race and I would lose. He had to be the center of attention even amongst kids, so once again my spirit was snapped like a no.2 pencil in a pencil fight. Why don't you race someone your own size MF! Soon one of my goals was to grow up and beat him in every way.

So with changing times my attitude changed as well. I was now a hardheaded boy with an attitude. I would fight my older sister and back talk my mother. I was very frustrated with the life I had. And I was getting at the age where my mother wasn't trying to whip me any more. So, guess who she called on to do the whipping? Yeah, you guessed it, it was my stepfather. He had a style that I didn't agree with. When he would whip me, I had to pull down my pants and bend over the chair as I got the biggest leather belt in the house. As I looked back at him begging for him to stop, he would have a force so tough it sounded like an F-14 fighter plane coming through the living room. All while the smirk on his face was loving every bit of it. Sometimes men love whipping kids who aren't theirs because it a way to show their true feelings through the belt. Afterward, I would look to my mom for comfort, but there was none. I was crushed and I began to hate them.

The frustration had really taken a toll on my mind and heart and I had visions of running away and or beating the hell out of someone. I'm glad I never had visions of murder, because the way I was hurting, I would've had all kinds of body parts in the basement.

But I continued to rely on the small joys of neighborhood friends, and all of the things we did. From the games we played like kick ball, high-water- low water, hide and seek, smear the queer, last tag, curb ball, dodge ball, pick- up jacks, all the way to the joys of the candy now and later, pixy sticks, squirrel nut chews, mike and ikes, jolly joes, boston baked beans, lemon heads, and push-up pops. These were the things that kept me walking the tightrope of insanity versus sanity and wanting to be a successful man one day.

I also had the joy of watching little brother grow, and at this time I had a little sister as well. She was a doll if I've ever seen one. My older sister and I never got along, but I couldn't tell if she felt what I was feeling or, if it was just me. Anyway, it was a total of six now in the three-bedroom double that we called home and I still had a lot of unanswered questions that I could only ask myself.

While everybody participated in being family, just by observing the family atmosphere, something was missing. Although we went to church as a family, to the drive-in from time to time, and to visit their adult friends and family, there was no love. It seemed to me now that I look at it, it was more of a job than a loving parent's responsibility.

As I watched TV shows like The Walton's, Little House on the Prairie, Partridge Family, and Eight is Enough; I wondered if that was really what life was like in the white world. It seemed that no problem was too big, and before the day was over, everything was okay with an ending expression of love. This made me somewhat envy the white race that I never knew, but yet be happy for them. This added more confusion to my melting pot of emotions. And before I knew it, I was wishing I were white.

These wishes were fueled, by seeing the lax attitude of the so-called head of the household. It was plain to see that at this time my stepfather was in way over his head. He had two stepchildren, two children of his own, and a wife that was some years older than him. He wanted to see what else was out there. It was plain to see that the house was being run by none other than mom.

So many things had added to the frustration that I was feeling: Wanting to feel loved and not just an unplanned child, wanting more family unity and communication, wanting more of what I wanted, wanting my stepfather to spend more good quality alone time with me, but most of all, wanting my real dad to get his life together so we could be together. I wanted a whole lot huh? No not really, just the things that should come automatically.

The Everyday Brother

Through these times my heart became more like, a fresh cotton ball that would leave behind tiny strands of cotton each time you wipe with it. My insides were tearing away and I became more frustrated every time I woke up each morning. I then began to blame my stepfather because since he came, things had gotten worse for me and the fetus of a monster was steadily growing inside of me.

I would often think back when mommy was a stronger woman coming out of a bad marriage. Her efforts were a lot different and she struggled for improvements. Even though the improvements were small, they were still improvements. Just like pennies they added up. I was happier and proud of my mother and what she couldn't do, my grandma Eva helped us. That was my dad's mother, remember? She would send my sister and I boxes of clothes, and money in cards just to say hello and she loved us. It wasn't the material part of it. It was knowing there was someone else who cared. It was like she knew my dad couldn't do it so she loved us for her and for him. She's at her resting place until GOD comes for her. I miss her.

When mommy re-married, it may have been a rebound that she will never admit to. I think he just wanted to capitalize on a pretty woman with a place to live. Because since then, all he brought to my life was arrogance, comedy, clean cars, and two children. The only thing I really loved out his package was my brother and sister. The rest of his package was like generic soda: all fizz and no flavor.

Sometimes as men we make things worse for others when we only think of ourselves. Coming into a ready-made family, we need to be more open-minded and think of the children who are the future. Not just about the woman, how she looks, how she makes you feel, or what's convenient for us at the time. Because even when we choose not to grow anymore, children are still growing. And they can only be what they're exposed to.

Mr. Cool, Step Dad, or Daddy, exposed me to feelings that I still couldn't identify. At this point, I didn't even know what I should call him anymore. I think I called him daddy because I wanted one. But in reality he was far from the daddy that any child would need. Most of the things he did didn't even include a young boy seeking a role model. He took martial arts classes by himself, which really hurt my feelings. As bad as I wanted to go, I was not allowed to. He would show me a couple of moves behind closed doors. More questions were in my head: Did he not want to be bothered? Was he ashamed of me? Did he really dislike me? The more questions I had the more steam I lost in my young life. I lived in a tug of war. My body on the outside lived one way, but my insides lived another way.

Still growing, I was observing everything that took place. I was still wondering how could a man be satisfied knowing that the children in the household went to bed hungry from time to time? Why was a growing boy only allowed one helping at breakfast, dinner, and snack time? Did anyone notice I was growing? Yes. Mommy knew but what could she do? It was obvious we had outgrown the family income.

As I grew, I noticed the look on mommy's face was turning into a scowl. We were in a light struggle and it showed. We drank powdered milk when that's all there was, syrup sandwiches when there was no meat, cinnamon and sugar toast for the sweet tooth, and the list goes on and on. It was plain to see we needed government assistance to help meet our needs.

WIC came into the picture, which stood for Women Infants, and Children. And yes that was us. WIC provided food products for low-income families once a week. They gave us milk, juice, cereal, eggs, butter, and cheese. I had never seen a block of cheese so big! But they made good grill cheese sandwiches though. WIC came on Wednesdays', and I would pray that the WIC man would come before I went to school so I could have milk for my cereal.

The Everyday Brother

All the while, daddy never had any feelings like he needed to step up and take things to another level. We lived on food stamps and he had no shame as a man. It was difficult to get a quarter sometimes for candy, which was really saddening. Mommy would send me to the store with some food stamps and I would have to bring her exact change back. The only thing I could do sometimes was look at the candy counter and dream of a zero bar or snickers. Then I would walk back to the cooler and wish for a cold Faygo pop or a freeze pop. Man, sometimes it was rough.

I remember one time after a heavy storm the rain washed a five- dollar bill in front of my house. I picked it up and thought I hit the jackpot. I told daddy of my new findings. Guess what he did? He took it from me and went to the store to get three sixteen oz. Pepsi's, a pickle, and a big bag of mike sells' sour cream and onion chips and brought me a $1.25 change back. As much as I enjoyed the thought of getting all the sweets I wanted, it was only a thought. And he didn't even take me to the store with him. This killed what little I had left in me. The monster in me was ready to give birth and take over my life. I wanted him dead.

A Different World

As age and hatred took over my life, it was time for more advancement. I was in Jr. High School now and I felt like I was really growing up. I was getting at the age when I really liked girls and sports. Even though I wasn't allowed to play in any organized activities, I made it a point to be good at football and running. Even if I had to play or run by myself until the neighborhood kids returned from football practice.

It was the beginning of the 1980's and all of the neighborhood kids were being placed in different schools by way of school bus. Even though schools were in the neighborhood, it was time for us to mingle more with the whites and vice versa. I don't think the whites liked coming to the east side. Desegregation.

My first year I got off scott free because for some reason, the school bus drivers went on strike and the school I was going to was out on the west side, which meant a slight delay on going to school. So I thought. Just because the buses weren't running did not mean I was staying home. So my mom enrolled me in Champion Middle School, which was a ten-minute walk from my house. I didn't know if my mom was ready for me to start my education on time, or if she just wanted me out of the house. But, because I had a negative attitude, I figured she just wanted me out of the house.

Champion was cool though, and I met a lot of cool people. Junior High School, or Middle School as they called it, was a little different education wise, because it was preparation for high school. I started off a little slow because I was caught up in seeing the new faces and checking out the girls. So I was a little distracted. Okay, I was a lot distracted.

The teachers taught well and they took pride in their teachings, consistency, and their articulation. If you weren't paying attention, they would call you out. So you know I was called out on many occasions. They wouldn't hesitate on telling you to go out in the hallway for two swats. In case you forgot, it was that piece of wood shaped nicely by the woodshop teacher to burn your butt.

After a day at Champion, I would walk home to what I would call reality. Soon all of the smiles I had all day would start to drift away and I would prepare myself for a different mindset. When I got home though, moms made sure I got on that homework. No matter what was going on or how she felt, she made sure I did my homework. I liked that in her because if she had no time for anything else, she made sure I got my education.

Oh, in case I didn't tell you, mommy was very intelligent and never boasted about it. She took time to read and write and was a master at typing and shorthand. She could even write perfect cursive and print both right and left hand. You know that word I'm talking about I just choose not to mess it up. The both hand word.

Even though I wasn't too fond of homework, this form of attention was good for me. It let me know that mommy cared about the important things. I soon began to realize that it was more than just me, she had three other children as well, plus that big headache she had. That headache was husband number two. She had other homework to think about and younger children.

Champion Middle School was a breeze, but living at home had its bumps. I could tell that moms was having problems in her marriage, but she struggled to keep things going because it was about making it happen for her children. My stepfather was still being cute and halfway selfish, not giving a damn about the young men in the house. He felt there was no need to be a positive role model, only a cute comedian.

My real dad would still continue to stop by from time to time to say his hellos and ask how we were doing. The more he came over, the more lies he told. I guess it was the addiction to the alcohol that made him see things the way he saw them. I never told him that I called Mr. Cool dad because to me he was still a walking time bomb with the liquid poison in his system. My disappointment was doubled because the men that had come into my mothers life were not beneficial only artificial.

As Champion was coming to a close, I felt like what am I to do now because the temporary escape from hurt, frustration, and bitterness would soon come into effect full time again, and I needed something to do to drown out these feelings. I didn't want to be home all day with nothing positive to do or think about because I knew that would only heat up more lava in my emotional volcano ready to erupt.

Summer came so quick it was ridiculous. I had basically the same routine. Summer camp, free lunch trips, going to the neighborhood swimming pool, or just playing around in the neighborhood. Mommy was working again and my stepfather was still working I guess, so sometimes I had to babysit my little brother and sister. Even though babysitting cut into my summer sometimes, it was teaching me to be somewhat responsible for my siblings. But honestly, I think if we could afford a babysitter, moms would've had one.

Even though there was work in the home, I was too young to realize that sometimes income just wasn't enough. This frustrated me because as a youth you just want your parents to get you the things you want without even being mature enough to see that parents who are the adults see the situation from the support end verses the receiving end. I say that to say this: money was still tight.

Even though things were tight, as a young black kid there are some things I would never trade for the whole world. Like the neighborhood kids, the games we played, going to the carryout for candy, and so much more. It was something about being on that thin line between broke and homeless that made life challenging and fun as a young boy. These things would put the monster inside to sleep for a while. I couldn't understand why happiness would come and go so much.

On the other side, there were some things that I would trade, like the men who entered my mother's life. I wanted what was best of my family, but I had no control or input on our family situation. I wanted so bad to grow up so I wouldn't hurt anymore, because I said to myself that I would never let my kids hurt the way I hurt on the inside. Truth is, I was partially damaged but not totally.

I had hidden dislikes that I didn't know how to express. And I probably knew I would get my butt whipped also. Since my stepfather liked whipping me with my pants down, I smiled in his face and flipped him off behind his back. I did that because I saw other pressures on my mom that didn't have to be there. She always took care of all four of her children, made dinner, and did house work. At the end of the day, she would sit down to her favorite entrée; Mike Sells potato chips and a big dill pickle. Most of the time she would send my sister or me to the store to get them with the food stamps. I was always told "Don't tear the five dollar bill out of the food stamp book or its no good, and bring all my change back!"

"Mom, I can't get nothin?" "No, because that has to last us until the end of the month." Sometimes this hurt me really bad because I was thinking: "Damn, I can't even get a fifteen cent Chic-O-Stick?" It took me a minute to get the importance of food stamps through my thick skull. Even though it wasn't real green currency, food stamps were an important part of our lives. Its how we ate!

Even though I wanted candy benefits from the food stamps, believe it or not, I was a little ashamed to spend them in the carry out in front of anyone. If neighborhood friends were in the store, or a pretty girl, I would wait until they left to pull them out of my pocket. I would travel the store pretending to be undecided until the store was empty. Sometimes I would even walk down the street to another store if there was a crowd. Being ashamed turned into anger because I felt we should have more with a man in the house. Especially if you thought you were all that.

It pained me to see that the head of the household was basically getting away with murder to my young eyes. Even though I didn't know everything that was going on, I knew a lot. For one thing, I knew that mommy wasn't holding him responsible for much of anything around the house. I'm not trying to put him down, but sometimes you have to make a man step up to the plate, if not, he's only going to do the minimum and no more.

To me, the minimum was all he did because we helped mom clean the house, hang the laundry, and I was in charge of taking out the trash. Man, I used to be mad because the trash man would come around 5:30 or 6:00 in the morning. I could hear my mom calling me: "Man, I hear the trash man down the street so get that trash out!" My first thought was always; why can't he take the trash out? And to my young developing body those trashcans were heavy. You remember the metal trashcans? Maaaaaaaan sometimes I thought they weighed a ton, especially when they got water in them. I would've liked it more if we did it together. I wanted him to be closer to me and to show me more attention. I really craved that male role model that I was looking for.

My crave continued because I don't think he was feeling me. I had a love for him, but I had a hate for him as well. You know how that love hate thing goes. I loved him because he was there, my mom loved him, and he loved his children. I still loved that coolness about him also. But what I hated was the fact that he didn't really come through for me on most occasions.

I remember when I used to beg him for a bike but it never happened. The first bike I ever had was a used pink girls' Huffy with a busted seat on it and you could see the foam coming out of it. Not only that, I had to share it with my older sister and it was a Christmas gift. And it was even under the Christmas tree like it was brand new! I was confused because I didn't know if I should appreciate this or not. Was this sarcasm, laziness, or were we that broke? And to top it off, it came from the pastor of our church his brother!

The situation didn't go unnoticed though, because my uncle June Bug built me a truck bike of my own. He even spray painted it and everything and it was the sweetest truck bike around. Even though everyone else was riding a Huffy and ten speeds, I was sporting the hell out of my truck bike. It hurt me that behind my back the neighborhood kids would laugh at my truck bike, so most of the time I rode by myself. But it hurt me more that my mom or dad couldn't afford to buy me one. Later, my neighbor J Wooden built me a BMX and sold it to me for $2.50. I also hated when people felt sorry for me. I also think the reason why I was such a fast runner was because I had to petal that truck bike. They were hard to pedal remember?

Even though I was unhappy, I tried to enjoy the low class improvisations that were handed my way. I was too young to feel the way that I felt, but I tried to cover those feelings and deal with life like a young boy should. I think it was because the wounds that I had did not heal properly. From the beatings that I saw my mom receive, up to the butt naked whippings that were handed to me by a man who wasn't my real father, I was going sour. But then again, real father or not, the butt whippings shouldn't have been with the pants down.

Like I said before, I wanted my life to be different, I wanted what I saw on TV. I was so sure that there was something better for me out there to take all the pain away that I felt. It had gotten so bad I would hope someone rich, with no kids would see me walking to the store and see the sad look on my face feel sorry for me and take me away. Little did I know all I needed was a good motivated, positive male figure in my life. That would kill any hopes of being taken away from my mother.

The temporary ups and downs continued in my life, and every morning I woke up I expected it. Physically I enjoyed being a youth, but mentally and emotionally I felt like I had suffered 80 years of inner hardship. Still time with neighborhood friends were the best and for the most part, they were living a life similar to mine. But I don't think they felt like me on the inside. I needed a certain kind of joy.

Even though I longed for a certain kind of fatherly joy, I took joy in seeing the smiles on the faces of my younger brother and sister, playing with them, and being Mr. Standup Comedian. My older sister and I fought a lot and most of it was my fault probably. I think I felt she got better treatment than I did, so I would do things to annoy her like go in her room to read her diary, mess with her toys, and so on. She had this model Corvette that I loved and when she was away I would go roll it across the floor like it was mine.

I can remember being upset with my sister for a long time because she used to be in the Big Brothers Big Sisters Program and she and her big sister would go on special outings and events. Her big sister was a slim white lady who I had a slight crush on, who treated my sister with a lot of respect and made sure she enjoyed her outings. She had this live powder blue Volkswagen love bug that I would die to ride in, especially with her. I had daydreams of riding around with her all day eating Chic-o-Sticks and Now and Laters rubbing on her pale white legs. I told you I was a young nasty since kindergarten remember?

But why was I mad at my sister? It wasn't her fault at all, so I shifted my sour feelings to my mother because she made the decision to put my sister in the program. Even though I was younger at that time, I had strong enough feelings and enough sense to realize that I was the one who needed to be in the program. I was the one who needed a big brother to comfort me, take me on special outings, someone I could model myself after. She was a girl who had mommy to relate with right? That action along with others led me to believe she got first class treatment. Sometimes I thought my mother said the word "no" to me just because I looked like my father.

I once read in book by a psychiatrist, that by the time we turn 18 years of age, we are told no more than 148,000 times, so that's what we become so used to and it puts us in a negative mindset to later say no even when we may want to say yes. "Mommy can I stay outside longer?" No. "Mommy can I have a quarter to go to the store?" No. "Mommy can I have some new shoes?" No. Mommy can I go swimming?" No. I believe I may have doubled or tripled those numbers. I think they surveyed the upper or middle class people on that one.

But I didn't get the word "no" all the time so that was a good thing. But you do get them more than average if you don't have much as a family. Sometimes I got things even when I didn't ask like new shoes, a new shirt, or whatever. Sometimes there was even and extra reward with going to the drive-in on weekends. But for the most part, that came when it was necessary like the shoes and the shirts and things. The movies were splurges, an added reward for a good week as a family I guess.

The Everyday Brother

Do you remember the drive-in days? Man that was a deal if there ever was one! You could go to the drive-in with a full family carload for five dollars plus you could see about 3 movies. Preparation for the drive-in was like preparing for a family reunion or something. Mommy would make popcorn and put it in a big paper bag, a jug of cherry kool-aid, and other little snacks. Oh, and don't forget the blankets and pillows, because when we got there, the only thing we needed to use that belonged to the drive-in was the restroom. We couldn't even think about going to the concession stand!

Coming up the way I did, meant that things were tight sometimes, but we enjoyed every minute of it because families made due with what they had without any further spending. But what I enjoyed most was the family time and I loved those days when dad would take us on outings like that. Sometimes I would just watch him drive being proud that he did this act of kindness and I would silently thank him from the back seat of the car.

I still couldn't understand why happiness was so temporary. Was it me? Yes, it was me, because I noticed that my feelings had no boundaries as to where they were going to end up. As a youth was it wrong to want to be happy all the time? Did I deserve that? Well if I didn't that's what I wanted. I wondered time and time again if my friends felt the same way I did. Did they hide it like me? If they did, I would never know right?

I still received visits from my real dad and it seemed that nothing was changing. His addiction to the streets and alcohol had increased, and the lies became grander. He would always give me money then take it back five minutes later. I didn't know if he was trying to impress me, or if he just didn't know what he was doing. My disappointment in him never left only increased as time went on. I still wanted badly for him to fill that fatherly void in my life, but the more I saw my stepfather the more my father disgusted me.

Something in me wanted to take his life so I wouldn't be miserable. You hear me? Not to put him out of his own misery, but to take me out of mine. What was I turning into? Wanting to extinguish my own flesh and blood so I wouldn't hurt anymore? I just felt it would be best because I still had clear visions of the past. And as you know sometimes it's hard to put the past behind you without proper healing time, or in my young case, comfort and communication.

At this point, my stepfather had begun spending a little more time with me. He would come out and play football, we would go to play basketball, he would take me driving, and even went to a wrestling match. What I really loved most was we always went to church together as a family. And the more we did these kinds of things, the more I wondered why my real father couldn't be doing these things. And the more I wondered, the more I hated him for what he did.

Even though I was slightly pleased, I didn't forget the butt naked whippings, and having my first five dollars taken from me. I didn't forget the special meals that were prepared for my stepfather as I got to eat the minimum bowl of cereal and the only extra I received was if he was full. At what point do you say "Baby make some for LittleMan too, cause you know he loves pancakes!"

Pancakes to me were the breakfast of champions. When mommy did fix some for us I felt special. It was like wow! No Cream of Wheat or cereal today, it's only the finest of breakfast foods. I used to stand by the stove sometimes to wait for mine to come off the skillet. Then mommy would say " Man, get out of the kitchen until I call you!" And when my two cakes were done it was on! I was only allowed two because that was what our family budget allowed, but those cakes along with some Karo Syrup made me feel like a king.

It was painful sometime being a growing boy and only allowed so much to eat and you're still hungry. I had to do something about this. But

The Everyday Brother

what could I do? I had to get a job because I was getting bigger and I needed more as a young boy. I wanted a paper route, my friends had routes, so I figured that would be the best thing to do. Simple right?

One day I approached my friend who lived across the street and asked him about his paper route. He gave me all the details and even asked me if I would like to go deliver with him the next day. I accepted his offer in a hurry because I was curious to know all the details before I approached mommy with it. I always saw him take time from playing to go deliver his papers in the afternoon and I admired that he had his own little job with the ability to have his own candy and toy money.

As the next day approached all I did was vision doing my own work and saving up for the things that I wanted most without waiting until my mothers' finances allowed it. I went with my friend and he showed me the ropes like a pro. He told me about the importance of neighborhood news and how important it was to get the paper to the doorsteps in a timely fashion. I thought this task was very easy for a youth and I was ready to get my own paper route and start as soon as I could. He even introduced me to his route manager and explained to him how good a paperboy I would be. The man said all I had to do was talk to my mother because he could really use me.

As I got my strategy for my proposal together, I decided to ask my stepfather first since he was the cool one and all, I thought he might think it was cool of me to want my own little permanent job. When I approached him with it, he just said: "Ask your mother." You see that was his way out of it and once again there was not much support from the man of the house.

Now it was time to approach mom with it. I had to change my approach to a more pitiful one since she was the mother, you know it's the woman who's supposed to be more sensitive and understanding. As I went to the kitchen with my approach, I saw the look in her eye that she didn't want to be bothered. But to me it was now or never, so I tried to control my stutter as I made my proposal. Oh yeah, by the way I stuttered a little or sometimes a lot but I made it through. I think it was from childhood mental stress. Anyway, after my proposal was finished she looked at me and said: "No, because I would have to be responsible."

My world was crushed as I said no more and went across the street to tell my friend of the bad news. He said not to worry and I could go with him sometimes to deliver papers, even on collection days and he would even pay me to help him. I accepted the offer as I let his kind words extinguish the fire of frustration that I had in me.

News Flash! Today my younger brother is 27 years old, it's 2005, my mom is almost 60, and she helps him with his paper route! Do the math. Today is 9/11/05, happy birthday to me.

Today I'm not mad, but then I was hurt, confused, and bitter. I wondered why I couldn't do the things I needed to do to get some of the things I wanted. I wasn't allowed to play football, have a paper route, or any of the things that my neighborhood friends did. Since there wasn't much explanation behind it, I just assumed I wasn't liked much by my family. Do you know how that feels to feel unwanted sometimes? I couldn't understand why sometimes I was accepted and sometimes I wasn't. So I continued to dream and hope that one day an emotional tide would wash away these feelings.

Even though I was having a rough time, I was still happy for my friends. Especially my two favorite homeboys, Mike C and J Wooden. Mentally they kept me somewhat balanced on the tightrope of good and evil. Mike C, who was my homeboy since early elementary kept me laughing with all of the off the wall jokes. He lived on Oak Street not far from me. For the most part, we only saw each other in school and talked on the phone in our early years.

J Wooden was my neighborhood homie. I met him in my early years as well. He lived across the street from me. J Wooden was a high yellow brother who knew how to make money. You name it he did it. He sold bikes, had a paper route, and sold racecars. If it was something kids enjoyed he had it for sale or knew somebody who had it. J Wooden got me one of my first little jobs picking tomatoes on a farm for $5.00 a day. And we picked in that hot sun in the summer for that money. Now days, you can't pay me $5.00 to eat a tomato in 95 degree heat. But anyway, those were my homies. I looked to them to make my unhappy days happy.

For some reason I felt like it should be more to my summer than what it was. I felt like being told the word no constantly killed a part of me on the inside. But as a youth you never know the whole situation until you get older or get an explanation. What hurt me most was the times I asked to play football and was never allowed to do so. Every summer I would ask, and every summer I was told no. But mommy did break down one summer and buy me a football equipment set with the helmet, shoulder pads, jersey, and pants. What I would do was every time I saw my friends going to practice, I would go in and suit up and pretend I was going as well. But instead, I would go in the back yard and play by myself. You become good after awhile throwing the ball to yourself and catching it. But why couldn't I play with a group? Hell, I don't know either.

Even though summer was always a break from school, I never really enjoyed summer to the max. There were limits on my world as a youth. I only went to the swimming pool a limited number of times, had limits on the distance I could travel in the neighborhood, limits on how many times I could get a popsicle from the ice cream truck, and still had limits on home snacks: Two cookies. I had strikes against me; I was black, broke, and hungry.

I remember these pains like it was yesterday. Especially going to the swimming pool. Sometimes I would beg to go to the pool with my friends, and after 30 minutes of begging, I got one dime. One dime. After all that begging I was too exhausted to walk to the pool, but I gained energy when I got there. After a few hours of swimming it was time to go home. But wait here comes the ice cream man. Now you know after a long day of swimming you are starving right? Can I get some ice cream? Nope. I only had a dime remember? It pained me to see kids coming out with a dollar to cure their hunger. Most of the time if I saw a kid with a dollar I thought they were well off. When I had a dollar to my name it was by the grace of GOD on those occasions. I hated walking home watching everyone eating Bomb Pops, Push-up Pops, Ice Cream Sandwiches, and every thing else the ice cream man had to offer. I walked home hungry, frustrated and ashy. You know that chlorine made black folks ashy like we were in a powder fight. "Mommy, can I have something to eat? I'm hungry." "Little man, go in there and make you a half of a bologna sandwich and get two cookies until dinner time because ain't that many cookies left!"

The situation wasn't like this all the time, but most of the time it was. I can remember days I would search the ground for some change and had no luck at all. Sometimes I would find a few coins in the couch where it may have fallen out of dads pocket when he was taking a nap or something. But because I was honest and I wanted a mans approval, I would let him know I found it and he would just take it back. No reward or nothing. Man I got to leave this place.

You know, I was a pretty intelligent young dude and I found it hard to believe that times were that hard with two working parents in the family. I felt there was a lot of dislike for me in the household and I was only tolerated because I was that unplanned sexual act that happened in the course of young country love. I call it Average Black or Basic Black.

The Everyday Brother

Summer was almost at an end and I was pretty much ready to start school all over again. Even though I enjoyed the summer, my days were long at times because they were filled with sadness, bitterness, and hatred. Like I said before, happiness was only temporary for me because at the end of the day when my mind settled, a lot of unanswered questions rose to the top of my head like home made bread. As I prepared to settle in, sometimes I wanted to go to sleep and wake up to a new world full of loving parents, new clothes, and all the food I could eat.

One week before school started, I received a letter stating I would be going to Wedgewood Middle School. I couldn't get out of busing this time, because they weren't on strike, so that meant off I went to the west side. I was looking forward to it though, because I heard through some of the neighborhood kids that Wedgewood had a good mix of kids from different sides of town and it was a mostly white school. Even though I was partially excited, I knew I wouldn't fall too much into the back to school tradition of the new clothes and shoes.

For me, in most cases, because of the family situation I didn't get many new clothes for school, I maybe got one or two sets of clothes and that was it. Some years I didn't get any new clothes, or I got a new pair of shoes and no clothes. But mommy made sure I had my school supplies though, because again, she was all about going to school to get that education. As much as I told her about all of the latest items that were out, she always said: "You get what I can afford!" It was at that point I had to wonder: Is moms doing it all on her own with four kids?

As I continued to mature, it was plain to see that the man of the house was just a body posing for pictures. What I mean is he was playing house with the legal title of husband. I would even ask him: "Hey dad, can you get me some Doctor J's or some Nikes for school?" His famous words were always "I'll have to see." If I had a dollar for every time he said; "I'll have to see," I would've had Oprah Winfreys' money in the early 1980's.

I would even at times ask my real father to buy me something for school and he would always build my hopes up to the top of the rainbow and then the rainbow would disappear. Sometimes, I didn't think he would even remember the promises he made because of his condition. Even though he became an even bigger disappointment, I still had love for him. Emotionally, he was hanging on by a string with me, and I would soon lose all faith in the two men who I counted on, needed, and hoped would nurture me into manhood.

It was 6:56 a.m. and I'm standing at the bus stop waiting to go to my newly assigned school. As I looked at my neighborhood friends, who were always happy and eager to see school start, I felt a little awkward and out of place because I didn't fit the traditional mode of being totally new. One of the reasons black children were always anxious to see school start was because it was the time to get new clothes. It wasn't always the impatience to restart education it was the impatience of looking new.

Me on the other hand, I was 60/40. I had on new tennis shoes and socks, and underwear, a shirt that was brought by mom in late July, and some old jeans that were neatly pressed. I was real happy for every one else, and I complimented them heavily to take the focus off of me and the 2 other kids who weren't totally new. I even complimented the 2 kids who were worse off than me because I'm sure they felt like me, or worse. I felt I had to do that because when kids talk about you it can be critical and life threatening.

I got away with being cracked on because I was cool with everyone and even though I wasn't totally new, I was neat and good-looking, plus they new I was short-tempered and wasn't afraid to fight. Win or lose, I will punch you in the face, preferably the mouth. But anyway, I was happy for everyone who was new. So new they were stiff-walking.

As I looked down at my shoes, I felt happy, but sad. Not for me, but for my mom who did what she could to at least make sure her kids had something new for school. My shoes were canvas Chuck Taylors (Converse All Stars) that came from Schottensteins. Which meant if most name brands came from Schotties they were irregular, which meant there was a defect somewhere on the item. Which meant the front of the right shoe was bigger than the front of the left shoe. I tried to keep my feet moving so no one would notice but me. Because remember kids are brutal. Because if they noticed that one shoe looked like a Chuck Taylor, and the other shoe looked like a BoBo, it would've been on.

Man for me it was one of those days. When the school bus pulled up, it was brand new! Even the school bus driver was totally brand new! She was a small attractive young white woman with a neatly cut hairstyle, a colorful fall sweater, and some Lee Jeans. I used to love the way she wore those jeans too. As I walked on the bus being greeted by the rest of the neighborhood, the smell of new denim and vinyl seats made me sick to my stomach. But I had conversation all the way to school like nothing was going on. Once again I was pretending everything was okay.

The ride was somewhat long as we pulled up in front of Wedgewood Middle School. There was already a long line of buses there loaded with kids from other sides of town waiting to get off to greet friends they haven't seen all summer. We must have been the last bus to pull up because all of a sudden the kids flowed off of the buses in unison. It was like we all got off of modern-day slave ships waiting to integrate with our young white slave masters.

At the front of the school there were white kids and some black kids who lived on the west side who were already there. I concentrated more on the white faces versus the black. Some of the white faces said welcome, some said here we go again, and others said go back to Africa. Those were the faces I studied the longest and the hardest. Since I was already negative and bitter internally, my stare into their eyes let them know I'll accept you just as much as you'll accept me.

I also studied the clothes they wore as well. Most of the boys had on Levi jeans, Leather Nikes, and T-shirts that consisted of Van Halen, Motley Crue, Led Zepplin, AC/DC, and Molly Hatchet logos. Even though I had done little research on these names, I knew they were rock bands. And at that time to me, rock or hard rock meant anti-black.

The white girls had on Jordache, Calvin Klein, Sasson, or Lee jeans with Polo Shirts or nice fall sweaters. Their hairstyles were feathered cuts with a lot of hair spray. They had that bionic woman look about them that I thought was sexy. Don't get me wrong, some of the black kids wore these same clothes as well, all except the hard rock t-shirts. And the black girls were even sexier. At the time these were the top of the line clothes, and to me, these were the people who had a little money or at least their parents loved them. The rest of the kids were average but neat and new, used but clean, and then a few were just bad off.

Even though I hadn't been in the world but a minute, I had the gift of giving credit to those I didn't even know. I would smile and silently appreciate the black mothers and fathers who took the time to get the boys haircuts, and to the mothers who took the time to braid, perm, press, or install a jerry curl. Whether it was by Lustrasilk or Kiddy Kit, I enjoyed seeing it. I appreciated that in my own mother as well, because even though I didn't have the best of clothes, she made sure I had a haircut and was clean. But it still just wasn't enough.

Anyway, as my mind traveled a thousand miles a minute, the bell rang and it was time to go inside to my homeroom class. Wedgewood was a nice school with nice teachers. The principle was a black man, which I thought was cool, and we also had one of the coolest, meanest guidance counselors who could paddle hard. Together they tried hard to keep the school in order. Newsflash! In September 2005 the principle of Wedgewood was fired for allegedly having liquor in her office and performing sexual acts with another female teacher. Man, what's the world coming to?

But in the early 1980's the teachers taught well and hard, but it was up to us if we wanted to absorb it and keep it there. The first week was always easy because the teachers are trying to get to know the students, get seating assignments, books, and everything else. Turning in paperwork that needed to be signed by parents was a must also. Moms always made sure all paperwork was properly filled out. Especially the free lunch paperwork. If nothing else was turned in, that was the document that had to be turned in promptly. If moms didn't trust me to turn it in, she probably would've had it delivered UPS or FedEx.

After the back-to-school honeymoon was over, it was time to really get cracking on this class work. I was a pretty intelligent young man, but I didn't always apply myself. I got distracted with meeting new friends, the girls, lunch, and recess. I really loved recess because I got to show how well I could play football and run. What I felt good about the most was the fact that most of the boys played organized ball and I was one of the better young athletes in my class. Lunch and recess were really the best part of my day, probably because it was my chance to eat and play.

I guess at that time eating and game playing were always at the top of my list. Even though mommy preached education, she was spreading herself thin and the discipline was not always consistent. And when it comes to a boy, you also need a certain type of discipline from a man. Not just butt whippings and small gestures and actions to let you know you are just a stepchild. Without that, all I had was hunger and recess. It pained me to see that I could not get that much advice from a man in my family.

I could easily identify the boys in school who had fathers or positive male role models in their lives. They looked different, acted different and smelled different, at least I thought. I could even tell the boys who had maybe one other brother or sister or was an only child, because their attitude was different. They didn't have to struggle much to make decisions. But me, I struggled on a daily basis to stay focused.

I admired the students who could stay focused and get all of their assignments turned in on a daily basis. Not that I was a problem student or anything, I just struggled to stay on track because my mind was going in a lot of different directions. I was truly unhappy with my life and what was going on in it, and what had went on in the past. I say that to say this; on any given day I could be an A student or an F student, it all depended on where my head was.

Since my head was mostly everywhere else except the classroom on most occasions, I turned my focus on some of the students who seemed to have some of the same symptoms as myself. It made me feel a little more comfortable dealing with my own mental and emotional problems. This group consisted of boys and girls who talked during class, wrote notes, threw spit wads, was tardy, slept during class, and every thing else. We waited until the last minute to do homework and rarely studied for tests. I thought this group was cool.

There were also white kids in this group as well, and together we had our own little society. This was what I called my in-school group because when school was over it was back to the same life that I always had: Being the young bitter boy back in the neighborhood wishing my life was different with the same friends and the same hunger. My two worlds were all I had, and as my brain grew larger I figured if this is all I've got, I don't really have anything.

As I continued to be scatter-brained, bitter, and confused, I noticed that my mother was becoming unhappier. Some things were going on in the house that I hadn't really paid attention to. My stepfather was missing in action a little more, and I could tell that it was affecting my mom. He began to stay out late and at times I could hear them arguing and my mom throwing things. Through all of that, she continued to do the best for her kids without much assistance at all. It was difficult for her I could tell, but she held on to her motherly strength.

Her unhappiness made me become unhappier and I could tell it was all coming from her husband. Even though they argued and she threw things at him he never put his hands on her, or at least I didn't see it. I will give him credit for that. But she was still unhappy and that bothered me to the point where I just wanted him out. And besides what did I really profit from him as a young pre-teen?

Well I can honestly tell you not much of anything. And the more my mom held on to him the more I began to dislike her, because at that point in my life I was thinking if your wanted a marriage you didn't grow from in any way, you should've stayed with my real dad. That's why my anger grew like the plague. And soon that anger would become a freight train at maximum speed. Can you stop a train? No, a train can only stop itself. You know what I mean.

At this time in my life, I tried to stay away from home as much as I could, meaning I stayed outside a lot and I didn't come in until it was dark and the streetlights came on. That was my curfew and my mom used to say; "Man when the streetlights come on, I want you in this house!" I was never on time because I became real hardheaded. I was a boy remember? Let's do some math real quick: 1 bad father + 1 half ass stepfather = 1 hardheaded boy. In life terms 1+1 can equal 1.

I continued to go to school and do what I had to do as a middle-school student. The more I went to school, the more I saw new things. I saw kids that smoked cigarettes on the side of the building, I saw kids that were looking spaced out, and I also saw kissing and grinding. The kissing and grinding really caught my attention as well as the spaced-out students. I already knew what the kissing and grinding was about because I was a young nasty, remember? But the spaced-out look made me curious. Were these kids drunk? What were they getting into?

It was plain to see that these kids were way ahead of the game for their age. Were they like me? I wasn't sure but I was going to investigate.

Since these kids were mostly white, and a couple of blacks, I thought I would just get to know them a little better and see what the hell was going on. Through my investigation, I found that these kids thought I was cool already. They were a step up from the tardy, loud, spitball throwing kids.

It also seemed like these particular kids didn't have a care in the world. They didn't care what their parents thought, teachers, or anyone else who came within eye contact of them. They were their own rebels living life just to do as they pleased. Their attitudes were not hostile, but sly and sarcastic with no prejudice, only accepting those who had the same belief system as them. Color didn't matter.

It pleased me to see that color wasn't an issue, so a few of us black kids who cared about everything but being A students developed a mixed society with some of the care-free white students. We became the schools mediocre students who went to class and paid enough attention to just get by and make the passing grades. Even though I knew on the inside I was better than average, I chose to be average out of hurt and disappointment.

Home life was still the same and the more I grew the more I wanted to be someone different. I still continued to want the perfect male role model in my life who could see my needs as a young boy. Who would take me places where just the two of us could go and have a good time, talk about girls, sports, and most of all, the things I should or shouldn't do as a growing young man. I knew right from wrong, but I just wanted someone to guide me and not whip me butt naked over a chair if I stepped out of line. That really scarred my boyhood you know.

The pains of having a father who was an alcoholic, a liar, and a man who couldn't provide dried my heart up like a Sun Maid raisin. Then when my mother put another man in his place who cared more about how he looked than anything in the world, clogged my throat to the

The Everyday Brother

point where I couldn't even swallow life anymore. It was like I was suffocating off of my own hurt, or like I was chocking off of a gob of peanut butter.

To avoid these pains, I just wanted to fall into a deep sleep sometimes and wake up when these men died of old age and I arose as a grown man starting clean and unblemished. But that wasn't happening, so all I had to look forward to was going to bed waking up going to school and interacting with friends and classmates. That had to do for now because GOD hadn't planned anything different for my young life yet.

I continued to sail through life looking forward to the simple things that each day had to offer. Like checking out the girls, interacting with the boys, lunch, recess, and class work. Yes, in that order. My mothers' strong push for education faded slightly so that opened up a door to my new focus on daily living. She still checked homework, but it wasn't as intense as it used to be so I did it and left it on the table for her to see then shifted my interests on what the average young boy was interested in.

My interest in girls became stronger each day and I noticed myself being extremely flirtatious during class time and lunch. Oh yeah, especially during gym class, because the girls looked real good in the gym shorts. You remember the old blue gym shorts with the one white stripe going down the side? Yeah I thought you would. Them babies were tight too, not only that, the boys had to wear them also. What were they called? Ball Huggers? And if you bend over too far you could see the darkness right underneath the butt cheek on the black kids, on the white kids it was pink. Excuse me for being real. I would always remind the girls to bring their shorts for gym.

I really enjoyed school time because it was the most complete satisfaction I had in a day. Probably because I got away with being mediocre, and my hurt, bitterness, and hatred temporarily ceased for that 9 out of 24 hours each day. I also felt my actions would go partially unnoticed, so that added a little comfort in life.

My first year at Wedgewood Middle turned out to be okay. I was well liked and accepted by all kinds of kids with all kinds of minds. I was even liked by the teachers, which made me feel really good because I wasn't always a model student. But when they told me to chill out and get focused, I did so. They saw my potential because I had a memory like a computer. But because my mind was like a roadmap with many different interstates, I was inconsistent. My inconsistencies would soon become my best friend, but sometimes your best friend isn't always a good friend.

Summer to me was basically still the same. Free lunch program at CMACAO, swimming when I had the chance, playing with friends, summer camp, and every now and then we would go to Detroit to see my aunt and my cousins. I liked going to see my family because it was a good getaway and I enjoyed playing with my cousin Poobie. He had all of the toys that I wanted, especially the Matchbox cars. Man he had a lot. Oh, and I still wasn't allowed to play football. Ouch!

Also, by this time in my life I had really grown away from church, even though we still went as a family, all six of us, it wasn't the same. I was thinking GOD hadn't answered any of my prayers so why should I put my all into church. I was young, bitter, and didn't know any better and too caught up in my own young selfish hang ups to even realize at the time that without GOD there is no me, there is nothing. I was even a Junior Deacon and still went through things half-heartedly. From scripture to prayer I just wasn't feeling it.

I was glad that summers went by fast at this point in life, because it took my mind off of my disappointments. I was tired of both of my dads, mad at my mother for being with these men and not allowing me to play football, and tired of not having enough to eat. I really hated those hot summer days when I was thirsty as hell and was only allowed one cup of Kool-Aid until dinner. But my stepfather was allowed unlimited amounts, and he watched me like a hawk when it came to the Kool-Aid. Even if it was a small corner left in the jug and he wasn't home, it had to be saved for him. I couldn't understand the logic in the Kool-Aid jug had to be totally empty before more was made. But you know what? I felt like I was being watched even when I went to get water!

When school started again, I was a young zombie going through the motions in life that I had no control of changing because I was young and didn't have options. If I ran away, I would probably be worse off than what I was so I decided to stay and deal with it. Not that I was in terrible shape but to me it was bad. I mean there was no equal treatment in the house and as far as treatment was concerned, I was last on the list. But there were kids who were worse off than what I was so I had to tough it out.

Sometimes I felt all I needed was a gesture of love through words or a hug. Sometimes I just wanted to see that smile from my mom that I used to see when I was smaller. But all that blew away like a Florida hurricane only to leave behind emotional destruction after the winds calmed. Did she still love me? If so, why was it so far out of reach? Why wasn't I equal? Why was I just a job? Was moms' love just spread too thin in this family of six? It doesn't matter! Even on my fathers drunkest days he told he loved me then staggered down the street. There were no excuses!

On my neighborhood outings, at times I would go looking for my dad. I knew where he hung out at so he wouldn't be hard to find. Usually, he would be in areas where there was a lot of activity. Wherever there was booze, bootleg joints, prostitutes, or nightclubs, he would be somewhere in the vicinity. I would walk to several places in search of the man who played a part in my conception. I knew he would tell me what I wanted to hear; even if it was a lie. No matter how drunk he was, he knew how to turn a lie into the worlds' greatest fantasy. Sometimes when I found him, he was so drunk he wouldn't even recognize me. At the sight of him, I would run home so fast, I would try to make it home before the tears would reach my lips. I hated him more than I could even think about. He was in no position to rescue me. I should've been careful because I could become what I hated most.

My last year of middle school was interesting because I took things to another level. I was a B or C student that year, and I made honor roll a couple of quarters, was standing long-jump champion, rope-climb champion, my homeroom was basketball and tug-of-war champs, I had the second fastest 50- yard dash time, was MVP in the teacher vs. student basketball game. I had a good year on my right side of life.

On my left side, I still interacted with a variety of kids, one variety in particular. These kids were the ones who watched MTV on a regular basis, and were fans of true rock. I couldn't really get into the hard stuff, but I was a fan of Hall and Oats, Phil Collins, Michael McDonald and a few others. They loved Run DMC.

These white kids and along with a few of my close black school friends introduced me to certain substances. Illegal substances. They included beer, marijuana, speed, cocaine, and opium. I saw the crazy effects of the cocaine and opium, so I didn't mess with that stuff. I did indulge in the drink and the smoke though, and at the time, I thought who cares but me. We would cut class and indulge, or meet somewhere after school. I hid this well from my family and my other group of friends. I did this by keeping eye drops, cough drops, and mustard packs.

I learned to hide this well because I suffered much disappointment already and I didn't want to disappoint the group of people who didn't indulge or admired me. Especially my boy Mike C, he was one of my best friends remember? If Mike found out he would probably kill me or want to try some. I couldn't risk either. I really didn't want his mother to find out as well. She was like my second mom. Gloria worked hard to take care of Mike and his little sister Aleta, and she always wore the finest of makeup and had the prettiest teeth. She would disown me.

I learned to live two lives on a daily basis. I was a young black version of Dr. Jekyl and Mr. Hyde. I spent the rest of my middle school life drinking 40 oz. beers, smoking weed, and selling pin joints for a dollar and bags of green for five. I hid my earnings and product in the kitchen drawer in my bedroom. My bedroom was an old kitchen remember?

High School Low School

Summer was more interesting and I was getting older. In some ways I still felt defeated, but it was time for me to fight back. As I got caught up in the ways of the world, I still focused on someday being a good athlete, so I continued to run, play basketball, and play neighborhood football. At least when I wasn't sneaking a drink or selling some joints. But it was time to make a stand and the time was now. I was getting ready for high school and I needed to make a statement.

"Hey dad, you want to race me?" "I'm watching TV right now little man." "Aw c'mon, it won't take long." " You sure you want to do this?" "Yeah." "You remember what happened last time don't you?" "Yeah, I lost." "Hold on let me put some sweats on."

I went outside, took a deep breath, and tied my unlaced shoes. When he ran, he always ran barefooted, I guess it was a southern thing. When he came outside, he stood at the top of the porch like he was King Kong, he had on hospital scrub pants, no shirt, no shoes. "I think you're going to need some shoes today." " Naw, I'm, good, just get this over with.

Normally, the rules of racing on my street were pole to pole, but today I wanted more. Pole to pole was about 60 yards, but today I wanted pole to corner. 100 yards. "Let's go pole to corner today." "You sure?" "Yep." He gave me that look he gave the day he knew he had my mom. Remember the look I was telling you about?

We walked silently to the pole, and it seemed like I walked a marathon. We didn't even look at each other, as a matter of fact I walked in front of him. The burning on the back of my neck told me he was still making that stupid face. The smirk.

When we got to the pole, I looked at him like he just shot my mother, and cut my real fathers balls off. "Are you ready?" he asked. "Say it." "On your mark, get set, go!" I took off out the gate like Sea Biscuit on a pound of speed. At the halfway mark, I didn't hear or see him. Did he stop? No, I was going so fast, when I looked back he was working hard to catch me, but that wasn't happening. I knew I was growing, but damn, I blew his doors off. Race over, I won! I calmly looked at him and said; "I won." I gave him his signature smirk and started walking back to the house. Truth be told, I practiced his smirk in the mirror because I knew this day would come. No shoes, no shirt, no service.

"Hey mommy, guess what?" "What man." "I just beat daddy in racing." "I think I'm really ready to play football now." "Yeah, since you're going to high-school, I guess you're ready." My heart smiled finally, and I thought to myself: things are looking up for me. I kissed my mom and I went outside. The rest of the day was silent for my stepfather.

Guess what? Mommy also signed me up for a summer youth work program. It was through the Private Industry Council. We called it PIC. PIC was a work program for low- income youth to learn different jobs at different companies to give us experience for the future. From manufacturing to clerical, PIC was ready to help out the youth. I thought it was a great program. And yes, we got paid! It was a real job.

The Everyday Brother

At this point I could see mommy was working for her four children alone more than ever. This frustrated me more because I was really tired of no-good men. Even though I had only experienced two, that was two too many. And I really hated the fact that they were too selfish to understand that what you do as a father or father figure affects the children.

But anyway, I was glad to have a small job during the summer, because this was a small vehicle to get some of the things I needed for school and this would take a little pressure of mommy. Now I could get some of the tennis shoes I wanted, without being hassled about the ones mommy could only afford.

I had good jobs through PIC from driving a forklift, to office work, to mopping floors. This gave me early experience that I not only needed but, desired because I always vowed to never put myself in the situation I was in when I got older. In other words, I enjoyed work, and I worked hard.

I worked for PIC every summer through high school and it taught me a little responsibility as far as working for a cash reward. I bought things like clothes, shoes, food, junk food, and I would sometimes pinch my mom off a little. I thought I was grown.

After the summer work program, it was time for summer football conditioning and boy was I ready. The bitterness I had about not being able to play sports suddenly turned sweet, but I still had sour bones in my body. Football was good, and I was one of the faster, better freshman ballplayers. And I never even played organized ball! I learned the plays fast and was very aggressive, it was my desire to play football and I was doing it.

Summer practice was over and it was time for the school year to start. It was a much different experience because I went from being one of the bigger kids in middle school, to being one of the smaller kids in high school. To the sophomores, juniors, and seniors, freshmen were almost invisible. To my 140-pound frame, West High School was huge.

West high was just a bigger version of Wedgewood, it consisted of a good mix of students and everybody pretty much got along. But there were still a few who had bad home training and thought the white race was superior and any other color should walk around the school in shackles.

Being a high school student gave me a different sense of being and I think it was because 1: I was playing ball, and 2: I had my first full summer of working. It gave me a sense of accomplishment that I never had. Even though I felt a little better, I still had problems balancing my other emotions.

What made me feel even better was the fact that my mom was happy for my happiness. I couldn't tell if she was really happy for me or not, but at least she acted like it. I even had her take pictures of me in my jersey and football pants because to me, it was a dream come true so I had to get proof that this was actually happening.

My real dad was ecstatic because he wanted me to follow in his footsteps. Not the drinking part, not the streets, not the women, but yes, football. He was pretty good remember? When I let him know that I was playing, he started crying. I knew they were drunken sensitive tears, but at least they were tears of joy. We would stand in the front yard talking about fake moves and front and back steps.

I enjoyed this time with him because we spent more time talking laughing, and joking about the one thing we loved the most: carrying the football and hitting the ball carrier. You know what? Everything he taught me in the yard worked on the football field. No matter how I felt or what went on, I was glad I could finally connect with him. A boy always needs his father's approval.

Even though I was one of the better underclassmen on the field, I was still an average student in the classroom. Each class was 42 minutes long, and there were 9 periods to a day. It was hard for me to stay focused all day, because my mind was like a tree and each branch had something different going on. Even though I was living my dream of playing football, I still had issues that needed preventive maintenance.

Even though the intelligence was there, I was just letting it marinate on the back burner always being clouded by bitterness and doubt. To ease the pain, I continually thought about football and girls, the two things that could always get my attention at any time. Where was my push? Where was my role model? I didn't have one. My mind was like the mind of an able-bodied welfare recipient; I was satisfied with just getting by.

It didn't seem like it was a problem to my fellow classmates, but it was definitely a problem for me. I knew it was more to me than just my football skills and my charm with the ladies. I just didn't have the strength to reach deep into myself to pull anything out that was in me wasting away.

Part of the problem for me was the fact that I was not happy with my home life. I witnessed my mother go through another series of marital problems which really was about to take its toll. I watched her stay up late waiting and wondering where her husband was. I knew by her attitude and the look in her eye that once again she was ready to end another useless chapter in her life as far as men were concerned.

I really tried hard to not pay attention to the arguments, and vowed never to take action until I was old enough or strong enough to handle the situation on my own. I saw her hustle around to care for herself, two high school students, and two elementary students. I felt sorry for my mom, but yet proud of her strength to continue to handle her business. Was it by design that our black mothers go through so much hardship? Hell no!

As my mother drifted from her marriage, we also drifted from church. I knew for the most part it was probably because of the fact that the pastor of the church was the brother of mommy's second husband and maybe she just wanted to cut off all ties.

My frustration caused me to blame everyone including GOD for what we were going through, and I just wanted to be rid of the burning pain of frustration, not enough love and affection, and sorry men that walked into my mother's life.

Since we had one foot out of the door as far as church was concerned, it was easy for me to blame the one who created life, gave us JESUS who died for all the sins I committed and more to come. I blamed mommy for having me, I blamed my biological father, I blamed my stepfather, and I even blamed the pastor of our church for even having him for a brother. I was young and stupid.

As I sat and took a good look at my life one day, I asked myself what did I want to be in life? Who am I? I was told to ask myself this question by my English teacher one day, Mr. Connie Boykin. He was a black teacher who was powerful. His voice brought knowledge and his articulation was awesome. I admired him in my own secret way, and I wondered what his life was like outside of school. I was too frustrated and ashamed to tell him I needed a role model to guide me through these tough times. But at least he saw my potential.

Anyway, what I saw was a young man who was smart, handsome, funny, and a great athlete. I also saw a young man with a bad temper, who drank and smoked weed secretly, who had a powerful lust for girls and women. Since I was living on both sides of the fence, I figured I would choose one of each. I wanted to be a pro athlete and a gigolo.

The Everyday Brother

Since I was already playing ball and sexually active, I thought this would be an easy road to take. Yes, I was having sex, and I thought I was on top of the world. I used these acts to cloud the emptiness that I really felt on the inside, because it made me feel like somebody.

As a young man with somewhat of a heart, I felt kind of bad by the amount of pressure that myself and other young men put on young girls to have physical relations with us. We convinced them to kiss us, put our hands down their pants, grind on them, and penetrate them. I really wanted someone to tell me that was totally wrong, but since there was no one, I just did whatever I wanted to do.

My other pleasure was more positive and it could benefit me in a better way as far as my future was concerned. We were well into our football season and I was doing well. I played offensive and defensive back, and each game my skills were picking up.

It pained me though that no one in my family had come to see me play yet. I envied the guys on the team who's parents, aunts, uncles, or whoever would be in the stands yelling and cheering them on. Even the guys who sat the bench all game had family members there to support them. I just continued to play hard even though there was no one there to cheer me on but my teammates.

One game I decided to just give up on hoping someone would show up to one of my games. In the huddle the quarter back called my number on an option play. At this point I didn't want the ball anymore. Who cared if I failed or succeeded, but I ran anyway. It was a good run for about 12 yards and a first down. When I got up to run to the huddle I heard a voice say, "Good run little man, just cut it up next time!" I knew that familiar voice, so I checked the stands and to my surprise my father was standing there with a smile on his face.

"Hey Rommey, who is that man yelling at you?" one of my teammates asked. "That's my dad, he used to be a real good football player." They all smiled for me and I smiled for me as well. Seeing him at my game gave me a new energy and I ran like never before. I ran for more than 100 yards that game. He was proud of me and that made me so happy. That moment took my football skills to a whole new level.

We won the game and it was a true highlight of my season. I just wanted to be recognized by my family on another level and it happened. I was anxious to get feedback from the football star from West Virginia who knew football like the back of his hand. I wanted him to know that I did just what he told me to.

I was happy my father came to my game on the right side, but on the left side, I was very upset that my mother had not been to a single one yet. This ate away at me for a while, but if I took the time to think I would've realized these crucial things; I had a younger brother and sister at home, and by the way, little brother was born with a life-threatening disease that flared up on a regular basis, she had a job, I also had an older sister who was in high school, and last but not least; she was going through her second divorce.

Mommy had a lot on her plate, but she made sure I had new football cleats each year, and she never missed an awards banquet or parents night during my whole high-school career. I would always wonder how she would do it each year after my summer work was done. She had to make it happen for four children plus herself off of $3.85 an hour. Minimum wage in the 1980's was less than $3.00 an hour. And you know what? She never received one red cent of child support from either husband!

After thinking about our situation, I realized I shouldn't take a lot of this to heart, but how can I not? I was truly affected and

The Everyday Brother

infected with feelings that I should not have encountered at such a young age, but since my mother's selection in men failed her, my insides had no choice.

Through another divorce I had to play many roles: high-school student, babysitter, trashman, landscaper, and whatever else moms needed me to do. She did most of the landscaping though, because she had a green thumb. Moms would plant sunflowers, tomatoes, greens, and cabbage. I loved when she would pull the sunflower seeds from the plants and bake them for us and salt them. I admired those motherly things in her, but I hated the way she let those two men run over her.

I felt ashamed of my situation and continued to keep so much bottled up inside me, and not to be opened until later in life. The men in my life were a major embarrassment not to be talked about, but only seen when they came around. I went through high school just hanging on hoping not to be asked much about my home life.

Part of being ashamed was probably as a youth, I focused so much on what other students had. Like the shoes they wore, the clothes, and how much money they spent during lunch. While they ate the Suzy Qs', Honey Buns, and Swiss Cookies, I had the basic lunch with no sweets on most occasions.

I was on the free lunch program. This was for the low-income students. Each student received a book of tickets that lasted through each school day of the year. You were entitled to breakfast for the day and lunch. It was just the basic meal with no benefits for the sweet stuff. Then there was the reduced lunch program. It was the lunch tickets plus forty cents, and then there were the full–pay students.

It was obvious who was on what program by what we ate. I felt salty at the school system for placing a label on us low-income students by having us walk through the cafeteria with that big ole yellow foam plate.

Rommey Stepney Jr.

To me free lunch tickets were just like food stamps, and sometimes I waited until the line was empty to get my lunch. Just like food stamps at the carry out remember?

But as a high-school athlete, I received extra benefits from my fellow classmates. Along with my free lunch, I received snacks from the vending machines, plus additional sweets during lunch on most occasions. I hustled at least $2.00 a day from students, mostly girls who liked me, and fellow teammates. This included upper classmen as well. If you were going to show off, then I was going to reap some of the benefits.

I was never really teased about my income status or what I wore, but there were a lot of kids who were. I would sometimes hear students say to other students; "Man you been getting free lunch forever, y'all must be poor as hell!" Students who received this kind of treatment got an occasional pack of cookies from me or maybe even an extra chocolate milk at other student's expense.

I went through all of high school like this but, it wasn't easy sometimes being one way on the outside and another way on the inside. But I continued being the high school athlete that I always wanted to be never shorting myself on my athletic abilities, but always shorting myself on opening up to someone how I really felt. I think I could've been a better student-athlete if I would've done so.

Even though I wasn't living up to my full potential, and internally I was an emotional vegetable, I turned out good as far as performance was concerned. I received several athletic honors in football and track. Yes, I ran track too, and yes I was pretty fast. Running freed my mind from emotional trauma just like football.

Best Offensive Back, Best Defensive Back, District All-Star, Two Year Track MVP, District Champion, Regional and State Qualifier, Central

The Everyday Brother

District Champion, State Indoor Runner-Up Champion, Most Athletic of my senior class. These were some of the awards that I received. I was proud of myself even though I had no family support.

It really tripped me out that I had more support from total strangers than my so-called loved ones. Students and parents from other schools rooted for me faithfully. This took some of the pain away from looking in the stands and finding no one there from my bloodline. To me, the one game my father came to and the parent's nights my mother came to just wasn't enough for my spirit.

I had a lot of trophies, plaques, medals, and ribbons to back up these accomplishments, but the emptiness inside me would never leave. I just wanted a positive male figure to say job well done, what are your plans for college or something. Or even someone to say they would be there if I wanted to talk. Moms and me didn't talk much and I was almost out of her reach as a teenage male.

I also received numerous letters of interest from several colleges for both football and track. As I read the letters when they arrived, it made me realize high school was only the beginning. I did have a little support from a couple of coaches, but it didn't really phase me. What I needed was parental guidance and input to carry me through. I wasn't strong enough to listen to the coaches alone and make a sound decision.

I let bitterness cloud my sight of the future and I only wanted things that came easy. Thinking about my future was something I didn't want to look forward to. I felt in my mind I didn't have what it took to go to the next level mentally and emotionally.

I continued to hide how I really felt by hanging out and drinking, and messing with a lot of girls. I had a girl from just about every public high school and some suburban schools as well. I let Old E, White Mountain

Coolers, Schlitz Blue Bull, Wild Irish Rose, and Thunderbird take my fears and emotions for a swim on a regular basis. I also let my craving for sex and my sexual activity take over with full force.

The way I was living was not the way a teenager should be living and I knew that. I truly knew right from wrong, but when negative thoughts and feelings take over your entire being, you gravitate more to negative activities. That was me.

I think what made me feel comfortable about these things was the fact that a lot of people were doing what I was doing. Some people did it because they wanted to fit in, some did it because they hated their parents, and some did it because they were just like me. We were the troubled and lost who had no answers and didn't know where we were headed.

But anyway, high school moved on because time waits for no one. The closer I got to the end, the more fear grew inside me. I was feeling pressure from everywhere. Friends, coaches, and schools continued to hound me with the same questions; "What are you going to do?"

For a minute, I was ready to count college out because I suffered a serious neck injury in a football game midseason of my junior year. This pained me because it put more responsibility on my mom, not much but some. Here we were as a family with one parent and four kids, one halfway handicapped.

I was in Halo Traction for a little over three months, and this caused me to stay home. I had a home tutor, which was well needed. It took me away from girls and drinks, which allowed me to focus on the right things. I did well with the tutor and I felt the one on one was much needed. My grades improved drastically which boosted my confidence. I was ready to heal and get back to school to show my teachers the new me.

The Everyday Brother

When I returned to school after my halo was removed, I felt refreshed. All of my fellow students were happy to see me recover well, and most of the teachers too. I say most because when the tutor submitted my grades, my geometry teacher changed my grade from a B to a D. She played me like I was incapable of improving. That instantly deflated me.

Senior year came fast and I played football, returning with the doctor's permission. I played well and the letters continued to flow. I was afraid to talk to moms because I knew I wouldn't get much push or feedback. I gave all of my letters to my girlfriend to put in a scrapbook for me. Mom was going through motherly motions and still never expressed love, only expressing responsibility.

Life was about having one or the other. I had a place to live with no love under the roof. I had a daddy but no father. I had a mommy but no mother. I had to make a choice between a high school jacket, class ring, a class yearbook, or a little stereo. Two cookies, but no milk. So I ate my cookies, wore my high school jacket, and listened to music.

It was still a good year in many ways. I received Most Athletic Male Honors and I was in the top five for Homecoming King. My dude Mike G won though, and I was cool with that. Mike was the basketball star who was also the West High barber and most popular. Fade-em' up Mike!

I had to borrow a suit from my stepfather to wear at the Finalists Pep-Rally because I didn't have one. I borrowed one for the Kings' Dance as well. My friend Bill busted my bubble in school when he asked me, "Rommey why you got your dads' suit on?" I tried to deny it, but every one knew because I had the sleeves cuffed under on the jacket. I don't know how the hell I thought I could get away with cuffing the sleeves on a suit jacket! Thanks Bill!

Moms hadn't really changed because she was still making poor choices in men. She met this guy that shacked up with us. He didn't work or anything. He called himself writing a book and being a poet. What do you have to offer me as a young man? I didn't think so! I couldn't stand no good men. It was plain to see my mother's needs and my needs were so different.

Anyway, she had never been to any of my track meets. Out of four years she never made one. I hounded her about coming to the last home meet of the season. Just like football, I would comb the stands in search of that blood-related body. It was the final heat of the 100-Yard Dash still no mommy. We got set in our blocks then I heard "Man, good luck!" It was my mother and her boyfriend.

The top sprinters in Columbus were here at the Hilltop Relays, and I was one of them. On any given day one of us could lose depending on our start. I couldn't lose this final home event. All I could think of was the day I beat my stepfather. At the sound of the gun, I took off and before I knew it, it was over. I won! Mom that was for you and a portion for your new boyfriend. Thanks for coming. 9.6 seconds.

My father couldn't make it because he was recovering from years of drinking. I know it was a hard road for him, so I didn't bother him. I was just proud of him that he chose to follow the doctor's orders to quit consuming all that rock gut. Good job pops!

Even though I had years of unhappiness in me, I always wanted my parents to be at their best. I couldn't control what they wanted for themselves, but I felt if they had better lives so would I. I wanted my father to move on and improve his life, and maybe, just maybe, he would become a better father.

Even though my high school years were almost over, I could still use a good male role model to help me in making a decision in which direction I could go in preparation for the real world. I needed someone to help me, love me, and guide me through my fears and frustrations.

I was afraid to talk to my mother about much of anything serious, especially my fears and hurts. I just had a feeling that she just wanted me to do something. Not because she wanted me to be somebody, but because she wanted me out of the house. As I matured, I realized since my mother didn't have a mother she couldn't really give the motherly love and understanding that a young man needs. Her mother started a cycle that would not be broken. I didn't say could not, I said would not.

Since things were like this, I ignored a lot of the letters and phone calls from colleges. I gave a few false hopes on gracing their university with my athletic skills just to calm down the phone calls. I also didn't want to tell them that I hadn't taken my SAT and ACT test yet. And I also didn't tell them that I didn't have a clue.

I didn't receive much help from my senior Guidance Counselor either. I think I spoke to her only once during my senior year. And that was because she called me into her office to tell me I wouldn't make it to the Naval Academy.

Here's what happened. Since time was winding down, I decided to go to the U.S. Navy with my best friend Mike C. After the Navy, I would go to the academy where I would then continue to play football. The Guidance Counselor read it in the paper through a big write up on me and she decided to take five minutes out of her schedule to kill the detour I was taking to being somebody.

"Mrs. G you wanted to see me?" "Yes, I just wanted to tell you that you will never make it to the academy, because of your academic performance." "Is that all?" "Yes." "Thanks for telling me, bye."

Once again a dream was shattered and I was through with the world.

Graduation came and it was the final act of my high school years. It was a wonderful event with my family members and friends. I was happy to achieve this goal especially with all of the inner troubles I had experienced. I was still scared though because I would be leaving home without a lot of the tools that I needed to make it on my own.

It really made me proud to see my father there all clean and sober. It was something about him smiling and saying that he was proud of me. It seemed that my mother was more relieved than proud, but I appreciated all of her support and what she did for me as a mother. Even though I knew it was rough for her, I guess she did what she knew how to do.

Graduation parties were all over town and I tried to conquer them all. My focus for the next few days was to sleep with all of the girls I could before they went away to college or wherever they were going in life. See, my head still wasn't right but that was all I knew and all I had to go with was what I knew.

I received a lot of gifts and cards and felt at least liked if not loved. My mother had a special graduation gift for me. Guess what it was? It was a five piece luggage set made by Oscar De La Rente'. I acted as though I liked it, but to me it was a smack in my MF face. To me it said get the hell out with a smile. Okay. I'll prepare myself to leave. Stay tuned.

Decisions- Decisions

The decision to go to the military was one I didn't really want to make. My dream was to become a professional athlete by way of college. I was disappointed in myself and in my parents for not giving me the push that I needed. I don't think they realized the importance of guiding their children and loving them in the right direction was much needed.

It had gotten to a point where every time I looked in the mirror I hated myself. I hated the fact that I wasn't strong enough to make it on my own yet. I hated the fact that there was a possibility that I would be another wasted talent. In the C.O., (that's Columbus) there were so many talented athletes that loitered our playgrounds and walked our streets with no desire to make the best of their talents.

I prayed daily to my heavenly father to muster up a strong desire in me to find the will to live my dreams. I was so scared of becoming a nobody, and it got to the point to where it made my head hurt on a daily basis. I had to make the best of something, and I didn't care what it was as long as I didn't become a nothing.

As I prepared my long military journey, I tried to put aside all of my hurts and fears so I could enter into a new world. I wanted to rid my mind and heart of everything wrong I ever saw. I wanted to start as if I just entered the world at seventeen. That's what I wanted, but it was not the way it would be.

My last day at home was a tough one. In my mind I wanted to leave and to never return. In the airport, there was a crew of family and friends that I knew I wouldn't see for a while. It was painful to say goodbye to everyone especially to my mother, brother and sister, and my uncle Bug. Even though I had some hang ups about mommy, she still had the biggest place in my heart.

It hurt me even more when she told me she loved me. After seventeen years, I never heard the words "I love you" from her much. Why are you telling me now? Is it because I'm leaving? Do you know where I could be headed if you told me that more a long time ago? If you showed me more? If you gave me loving advice?

But noooooo, here I am going to the military because I felt there was no love, I felt you wanted me out, I felt you didn't care if I played college ball, ran track or not. Do you mothers and fathers know how far I love you can carry a young man or woman? I took the fast track to the military because there was no I love you! Yeah I love you too. Enjoy that no good man of yours who wanted me out in a hurry. Gotta go!!

While there was pain in my heart, I was suffering from some physical pains as well. From time to time, I would suffer from stiffness and very little motion in my neck. This was occurring for a while now since my neck injury in high school.

I never told anyone of this little problem, because it didn't occur often. And besides, I didn't want this to jeopardize any chances of having a future in sports. Even though I didn't say anything about my condition, it was quickly noticed in the military.

"Stepney! What's wrong with your neck son?" "Nothing sir." "When I say dress right, you dress all the way right!" " Yes sir." Since we got up so early I never had time to work out my morning stiffness. This went on for a while then I was sent to medic.

The Everyday Brother

After having x-rays taken at medic, the doctor asked me if I had any neck problems in the past. I told him no, but he asked me if I was sure, so I told him the truth about my football injury in high school. He just looked at me and sent me back to my unit.

Later, I was summoned by a higher military authority. On my march there, I knew I was in trouble because I felt it in my gut. When I arrived, I was called in an office to sit in front of a man with a very hard look on his face.

"Stepney, I'm holding here your x-rays from the doctor that say you have arthritis in your cervical spine." "Oh really?" "Yes." "This report also says that you had some broken vertebrae in high school." "Uh huh." "Why didn't you let the military know about this?" "Because I didn't want to be turned away sir." "Well Stepney, we can't use you in this condition." "But sir, it's not really a problem, only in the mornings when I first get up." "Stepney we can't use liars either in this military, you will be processed for discharge."

As my heart stopped for a minute, all I could think about was being shipped back home to nothing. Once again, I felt like I was nobody, and if I tried or not, I would just be no one to everyone.

When I returned to my unit, I tried to hide the pain in my heart by wearing a firm straight face. But I became transparent after so many letdowns and disappointments. The guys in my company knew something was wrong. I had orders to be transferred to a medical unit awaiting my discharge.

The medical unit consisted of a group of men with many different medical issues. From busted knees to fat bodies, we were all there. It was like I was in the land of the misfits or something. Once again I was among the unwanted, and just like the rest of the men I just wanted to be loved and be somebody.

I silently questioned myself at night, and after a series of questions I would beat myself up mentally. I knew there were things I was good at, but it seemed I was better at being a young nothing. I began to think of all of the kids back home who thought I would amount to something. I vowed not to disappoint them when I returned to the C.O.

When I returned home, it was like I never left. Everything looked the same, and the neighborhood consisted of the same people going to the same place. Nowhere. I don't know why I expected something different in such a short period.

I felt like a major failure because I was back home and I needed to stay with my mother for a while. I really hated asking her because my plan was to leave and to never return. I felt like I didn't have many options at the time because I was still lost.

At home, my half of the room was still the same that I shared with my little brother. I thought I would have a warmer welcome, but instead I felt like I was a burden. I remember my mothers words very clear, "Man you gonna have to find you a job or something because you're grown now, and grown people need their own place to stay."

I asked myself; "What about this grown M.F. that's living with you and not working?" He's doing the same thing he was doing before I left. Nothing! After two divorces you still making bad choices in men? Take time to get to know yourself and children before you go taking any man off the street to be your sleep mate.

I was once again hurt by her and her actions or non-actions I should say. Instead of asking me if I had a plan B, or did I want to try to take the steps to enroll in college and maybe become a walk-on, she said some mess like that. And that bum she was with had the nerve to tell me, "Man your mother missed you while you were gone, she sat on your bed and thought about you." Yeah okay, What's up? Shut up.

Since the pressure was on to find a job, I went into hot pursuit. I didn't have much to go on but my high school summer work experience, so I was turned away a lot in my job search. It didn't really bother me because I was used to being shot down like a 1940's airplane.

Mommy pulled some strings and got me a part-time gig at the drug store pharmacy where she had been working for awhile. I appreciated it and worked well to keep her good reputation going. I was a cashier clerk and it gave me experience in dealing with all types of people with all types of personalities.

The pharmacy was Jewish owned and located in the east side hood of Columbus. On Main St. between Wilson Ave and Ohio Ave. Right in the middle of all the drugs, drunks, and prostitution is where I worked. I liked working where my mother worked and it gave me a chance to watch her and protect her if needed. I was an 18-year old bad ass.

I also liked watching her work, because she took so much pride in her job. She was always pleasant and professional and never folded under pressure. I always admired that part of her personality, and I tried to place that part of her in me. She never complained about the pennies she made, she just worked and was happy she had a job.

Press Pharmacy was the name, and it employed mostly people from the neighborhood, and we appreciated it. I don't care what people say about the Jewish, a few of them put businesses in the hood to help us out. Yeah, true enough their pockets were getting fat, but at least they were there.

After working at the pharmacy for a little while, I got tired of walking to work. Sometimes I would ride with my mother if we were on the same shift, but that was usually one or two days a week. I decided it was time for me to get a car. But you know what? That $3.25 an hour wasn't going to get me much, especially on a 20-30 hour workweek.

I started searching again hoping my little cashier job would give me some leverage. On applications, I would make that little cashiers job seem like I was a CEO of a multi-billion dollar corporation. I would be saying things like; I was responsible for all of the money that funneled through the store, in charge of time and attendance, and even in charge of security. I had a mouthpiece like a brand new Susan B. Anthony dollar.

Even though I was looking like Donald Trump on some applications, it still wasn't working. I went for the big high dollar jobs and nothing less. All I had was a high school diploma and a lot of dreams to take the place of the dreams that I wanted to fulfill that seemed so far out of reach.

Those high-dollar jobs shooed me away like a one-week old fly at a family barbeque. I didn't have the experience to fly around the back way to get the meat. I went straight up the middle. Then in some cases as Ice Cube would say, "my skin is my sin."

I continued my search when I wasn't working, trying not to be discouraged. The discomfort I felt in my mother's house made me push even harder to make more money so I could get a ride. At this point I was kind of fed up with the disrespect people would dish out when I was serving them behind that little cash register.

One day on my walk through the neighborhood I ran into my old partner J. Wood. Remember him? He was the one who built my BMX and had the paper route. We talked for a while and split a 40 oz. of Schlitz Malt Liquor Bull. I told him that I needed more money to get a car and I needed more hours to get it.

Wood told me about his job at the local Children's Hospital and they had some openings on the night shift in the housekeeping department. He told me to come to the hospital on Wednesday and he would introduce me to his boss.

The Everyday Brother

I knew J. Wood was a man of his word, so I had no doubts about what he said. You know how some people say things and never come through even when they offer? Well, Wood wasn't like that, he kept his word when it came to me.

Sure enough, Wednesday at 2:30 Wood was there waiting with his boss. "Mr. G this is Little Man, I mean Rommey the one I was telling you about. He's a good worker and he's smart too". "Hello son". "Hi, how are you?" "Fine if I could get some good help on third shift, could that be you?" "Yes sir, it's hard for me to sleep at night anyway". "Good, fill out the application and we'll get you set up for orientation so you can start next week". "Thank you sir".

As I did my mental rewind, I sounded like a field hand trying to get house duty. Knowing good and well I'd rather be partying with girls all night than working. Wood helped me with the application and gave me details about the job. Man, once again Wood was true to his word.

As pharmacy duty came to an end, I prepared myself for nights. So that meant trying to sleep during the day and staying up at night. It wasn't really hard since I was young, but I knew I had to train myself to at least take a small nap during the day. And I also had to discipline myself to stay home because I was so used to running the streets.

I was hyped starting a new job, because I was hyped about getting a ride. Plus I was kind of tired of serving disrespectful people too. But little did I know disrespect was everywhere. All I was doing was changing the level of disrespect from 20 hours a week to 40.

My job as an environmental services person was gravy. All I did was clean rooms all night, which consisted of dusting, mopping, sweeping, and taking out trash. Environmental Services was the new name for janitors, custodians, or clean-up crews. Whatever the name, the game was the same, cleaning up after people.

I learned very quickly that in a hospital setting if you weren't a doctor, surgeon, nurse, or hospital administrator, you got very little love. Hospital service staff was identified by the color of their uniforms. The cleaning staff, oh, environmental services; I'm sorry, cafeteria staff, and patient services were all color-coded individuals. Mostly black.

It seemed like we were looked down on, and as a young man I felt like scum. I already had no self- esteem, but this made it worse. If they took the time to think, the hospital could not function without spotless surgery rooms, food for the patients, or proper patient delivery.

I knew that I was putting my young mind on hold, but what was I to do? I had fell into the trap of working without thinking of trying to get something nice. I knew where I needed to be, but I couldn't get there on my own and there was no one there to put a foot in me. A mind is a terrible thing to waste.

I worked my night job with passion because my mission was to get my ride. I also worked hard because hard work is what gets you noticed, or in my case at least keep the supervisors off my back. I also learned that hard work won't get you a raise until it's time for a raise.

While riding the bus one day, I saw the car that I wanted. It wasn't anything that was out of my reach for a young man, like a BMW or a Benz it was a Chevy Z24. Which was a Chevy Cavalier Sport Coupe. They were hot when they first came out and I wanted one.

I was a young man with a one-track mind. If I saw something of interest, I forgot about everything else. My thoughts of going to college and playing ball or running track were slowly fading away. I just focused on working to get something nice so I could just get around town.

I knew in my heart all I needed was a push from someone who was in a good position in their life, or at least on their way. But everyone I knew was doing the same thing; working just to get by, unemployed, or in the drug game. I still didn't know where to begin finding the people I really needed to be around, and I just wasn't going to approach any man in a suit or nice car.

Until I found what I needed, I tried to enjoy my job and move on with what's going on. It was kind of easy to deal with because I worked all night and slept a couple of hours out of the day. Mom was at work during the day, so that took a little discomfort away from my feelings of her not really wanting me there.

The rest of the day, I ran around town being a young man of the streets making sure I had a place in a world going nowhere. I say that to say this; my knowledge of what was going on in the world was limited, so I was just doing what I knew which wasn't much. I wanted badly to talk to my mother about what I felt inside, but since we never really talked seriously, I didn't have a chance. I wanted to tell her how I still had a chance at living my dreams, but I didn't know where to begin. I wanted to tell her I was scared and I needed her to take charge in directing me. I wanted to tell her I never healed from the separation from my father. I wanted to tell her I'm sorry on his behalf for what he did or did not do. I wanted to ask her; Do you love me? Do you see what I'm going through? As your son, do you understand me?

When I walked into the house each day, there was a small shrine of trophies that sat in the living room. I had to walk by them in pain because one part of me felt those days were over. I hated myself as I remembered the good athlete who is turning into a spoil of the earth. I remembered giving away medals and ribbons to those who didn't receive any. I remembered giving away awards to girls who liked me and just said good luck. Now I needed someone to have compassion for me, I needed someone to reach down to pick me up.

After high school, family and the rest of the world classifies you as a man or a woman. Even though I hadn't been through much of anything, I was classified as such. I always wondered why some people were so quick to say, " I can't wait until I turn 18," because they were ready to either turn you loose or quit paying child support. So here I am, 1/8 of a man.

I realized working my night job was the only thing I had, because even though I was staying with moms, she had cut my cord at marriage number two. She just carried it in her purse the rest of the time pulling it out and wrapping it around her waist on occasions. I can still hear her voice ringing clearly; "Man, I did the best I could do for you, get over it!"

I appreciated moms allowing me to stay with her, doing the things that she did as far as clothes, food, and sometimes a few laughs. But I missed the part of emotional support, helping me to believe in myself, helping me to pick up and put together missing pieces that I needed to move forward in life. I knew the men in her life couldn't do it, so I relied solely on her. Was that fair? I wasn't sure.

I continued to work with uncertainty hoping a miracle would take place. Waiting on that miracle, time flew and I had saved enough money for a down payment on the car I wanted. After I got paid, I would pinch mom off some money for allowing me to stay there, kick it a little, and put some to the side.

After a long night of work, I decided to take a short nap and wake up to take a journey to see if the car I wanted was still at the car lot. I jumped on the bus on this sunny summer morning keeping my fingers crossed for luck. Sure enough, there it was, I was determined to get that car.

The lot was loaded with salesmen awaiting potential customers so they could put the rush on like a linebacker to a quarterback. They all saw me get off the bus, because it was right in front of the dealership. I walked right over to the car I wanted without hesitation. The salesmen looked at me and smirked and whispered as if to say; this boy rode the bus just to look?

I waited patiently then I decided to break the ice in my most professional voice." How are you gentlemen doing today?" "Better than most people" one replied. After no one budged, I figured it was hard to break ice from an underwater glacier.

My inner question was this; how in the hell can you be picky or discriminate when how you pay your rent or mortgage, how much you eat, how you do anything is based on how many cars you sell? If it's like that, why are you out here being a solicitor at your own place of employment?

I finally decided to go inside, and the first person to speak would be the first person to get the commission. "How are you today young man?" "Fine sir, how are you?" "You like that car out there don't you?" "Yes sir, that's sweet, what's wrong with it, it's been there for a couple of months?" "It's in good condition, it's just been waiting on you?" "Give me your license, let's go for a ride." "Cool"

The ride was good as well as the conversation. When we got back to the dealership, I showed him enough money for the down payment, plus insurance, plus enough money for three car payments. I learned early as a young black man you had to show a little extra whether you're used it or not.

After the deal was made, the salesman said he would have it detailed real good, and I could pick it up tomorrow. I felt real good about this, and it gave me a sense of accomplishment as far as working toward a goal. But you know what? I had no idea of what my next goal was, and I couldn't really think past the fact I just purchased a car.

Even though I needed to set goals and plan ahead, the only thing I planned was cruising the streets and picking up girls. Even though I had a girlfriend at the time, I saw a lot of pretty young thangs walking down the street or cruising that would look real good in my ride. I was all about trying to impress someone because I wasn't impressed with myself.

Not only was I pleased with my actions, so were a lot of other people. I was so simple-minded thinking a nice shiny car made me who I am, and the public was the same way. It seemed that my number of friends increased all because I had a car. In my world, friendships were based on what you had, not what you wanted out of life, or if you were in college, or had a good-paying job. It was all about what you drove around town in or what kind of clothes were on your back.

I used my car to boost my self-confidence and my self-esteem because I was low on myself. Since the car brought me a lot of attention, I took advantage of it. I took advantage of a lot of young women because all they wanted to do was ride around town and look good in my car. But you know what? If you were riding in my ride, there was a price to pay, and you would pay with sex.

I wasn't the only young man doing this though, a lot of us capitalized on the attention that we got from the ladies just from having a clean sporty ride. My motto was this: If you get in, you must sin. I had no regard for my own body or anyone else's. I never paid any attention to the fact that my body was valuable, and so were the young women I was violating. I was giving up my valuable juices with no love, commitment, or emotion. I was putting a lot of miles on my young body with no tune-up or proper body maintenance.

I knew what I was doing, but for some reason I didn't care. I was a young man and I knew right from wrong, but I let my bitterness cloud

The Everyday Brother

my judgement and only looked one way. On the inside, I was still mad at the world for not helping me make the right choices, so doing the things I did was my poor excuse. I was a solid case of how bitterness could easily turn into ignorance.

"Rommey, when you come over today we need to talk." "About what?" This was my steady girlfriend talking. My first thought was she found out I met some girl down at Franklin Park, took her home, and slept with her. "Okay, I'll come through before I go to work tonight."

Franklin Park was on the east side of the city where most of the black people in the city met on weekends to mingle, meet, and show off. And yes, I was a part of that crowd. I was real surprised at how I made a name for myself so fast and so early in the game. The young ladies came in packs and the men came with high-gloss on the rides and tires laced with armor all. I was one of the younger ones and was determined to be a heavy hitter. That's what I thought the conversation would be about.

"Hey, what's up baby?" "Nothing." "What's wrong with you, why you looking so sad?" "Rome, do you love me?" "Baby, you know I do." " I'm pregnant." Now, what's the next thing a young knucklehead brother would say to break a woman's heart? "Is it mine?" "Who else could it be?" "Hell, I don't know where you are when I'm not around." I would say anything just to throw my responsibility out the window.

After I was finished shifting blame, I thought how could I mess up the life of this young, beautiful, hard-working, college woman. Just because my life was put on hold by bitterness, hurt, confusion, and the streets I had to affect someone's life that was trying to make something of herself. Sadness rushed through my body like electric shock.

I thought I was halfway smart because I had a punk High School Diploma. In reality I was an uneducated, misguided fool. All high school taught me was the Civil War, Romeo and Juliet, a few numbers that I never use on the job, and how to make a birdhouse in woodshop.

I was never taught good consistent behavior, waiting until marriage to have sex, how to interview on the job, the importance of education, or respecting myself as well as others. But you know what? I can't blame the school system totally either. So what do I do? Whatever came easy, and whatever I saw.

As far as being a new father was concerned, I would not yet follow the pattern of my family members. Meaning I wouldn't be a young father just yet, there was another option. Even though I didn't agree to this option, it was out of my hands. Just because I planted the seed didn't mean I had any say so at the time.

My girlfriend decided that it would be best if we didn't have the baby. And as long as her mother was paying her bills and paying for her to go to college, a baby would be more than she could handle. I had to respect that, but I didn't believe in fetal termination. Or that word I hate, abortion.

Was it right? No. Was the time right? No. But this is what happens when young people jump way ahead of themselves and their own lives aren't together. Doing irresponsible things because it feels good physically. What I learned behind this was, if it feels good physically as a young adult nine times out of ten, the end result doesn't feel good emotionally.

I continued to do the same thing and get the same results. I had no problems with doing the minimum, and the only maximum I was getting was having fun. But the kind of fun I was having wasn't really fun, I was just blinded by the ways of the world with no vision of the future.

The Everyday Brother

Having all this fun was a camouflage to keep my fears unrecognized, because what I really wanted to do was become someone of major importance to the world. It was hard for me to talk to anyone about living my dreams because if the people I was with didn't have a vision, do you think they were going to support mine?

I was caught in the trap early of working to pay the bills and having fun with the rest. That was all I knew, all that my friends knew, all that our families knew, and all of their friends knew. I guess it fit the saying; when in Rome, do what the Romans do. But in reality, it frustrated me that I was working like a dog for two weeks to get a check, and ended up spending it in three days. It just didn't add up.

My frustrations, fears, and hang ups were mixed in together like vanilla and chocolate marble ice cream, and soon I wasn't able to identify who I was at all. I was a piece of flesh in this world only going places I was accepted, which meant I wasn't going too far. And I continued to do what every one else did, not having a voice of my own, only listening to other voices. And some of those voices were saying; "Rome you know what crack is man?"

I hung around many different groups of people, and they introduced me to some of their people. I was amazed at how many different groups of below average people there were. One of these groups introduced me to crack cocaine and took me on a grand tour from the kitchen, to the streets, to the big ballers. Man, this was some heavy stuff!

Fortunately, I was introduced as a distributor, not a user. To me, GOD was only going to let the devil take me but so far in the game, he knew I wouldn't be able to regroup if I was on the flip side of it. But it was really something the amount of damage this little rock could do. Next to the fear of not succeeding in life, this scared me.

As I cruised the neighborhoods looking to ruin more people's lives, I knew this wasn't where I wanted to be when I look back in the days of my innocence. I would sometimes think to myself; what if this person was my mother, father, sister, or brother? How would I react if a young man was out to ruin their lives with drugs? Knowing me, knowing the rage I had bottled up, I would have body parts everywhere. Dahmer style.

But, since it wasn't going that way, I decided to be an addition to the world of no-good men who poisoned the world. This drug made Christians stray, turned parents into deserters and thieves, young talented men into robbers, and young women into prostitutes. I was responsible. I was the source of innocence turning into devilishness.

And with my help of adding to the destruction of young black lives, I had the nerve to say; "These people were already like that, it was already in them, they don't want anything for themselves." This was my outer shell talking, because on the inside I had a heart. I felt sadness inside. Father GOD, please forgive me.

I wanted to make a change, but I was still struggling to find a beginning. By this time a couple of years had flown by, and my mother was frustrated with me. She saw me age, and I was just taking up space her in her home.

"Little Man, next week I'm moving and it's a smaller place for me and your younger brother and sister." "So what you saying moms?" "Baby you gonna have to find you a place to live." "Oh, okay that's cool." "The lease is up next week, so you have a week to get your bed and you clothes out."

In reality, this really hurt me but I guess I had it coming. For my parents everything was about age and nothing about teaching. But what could they really teach me? I had to get it myself, and just as I put time into the streets and women, I could've put time into finding myself. I say that to say this; age wise I was a man.

The Everyday Brother

What really tripped me out was, on moving day guess who helped her move? My father, and my uncle. Yes, the man who did my mother so wrong as she put it, did nothing for his children, helped my mother move. This is how I saw it; both my parents pooled together to leave me homeless!

As I thought about this, I gave them very little help. My thought was this; y'all were never happy together, now all of a sudden, y'all happy? Yeah whatever! As the truck pulled off, I said to myself I knew y'all would leave me hanging!

As I sat in the empty duplex, I realized this was all I had in life; a cot for a bed and two laundry baskets of clothes. This is all I have, this is all I have. I kept saying this until it really sunk in. And when it sunk in, I was furious!

In my fury and rage, I looked over on my cot and saw a note. It was from my mother. What the F is this? A Dear John letter? Yeah, it was something like that, it was saying how she did the best she could do for me and it's time to move on. She even had a quarter taped to the letter so I could call her so we could talk. I thought to myself; can a quarter buy a bullet? I've already asked the lord to forgive me for that thought back then so don't trip.

As I reminisced about the fancy cars and the good times, I cried and bit my lip until it bled. I thought about all the fun I had, cruising the streets, the ladies, the parties, everything. It was all gone, and without the cot and two baskets of clothes, I would be back to where I started at birth; butt naked and full of tears.

I called my mother from the phone booth beside the carryout I would walk to as a little kid. She told me that she talked to my father and I could stay with him until I get things together. My first thought was; I don't want my parents to feel sorry for me, I want you to teach me to be better than you. Isn't that how it should be? Don't we want our children to be better than we were at that age? I thought so.

As I hung up the phone, I looked around the neighborhood, and thought, this is where I grew up, but it doesn't have to be where I'll end up. So I agreed with myself to stay in this until I could get out and just live with caution.

I picked up a piece of glass, cut both my index fingers and made a pact with myself. Someday somehow I will get it right no matter how long it takes. I became my own blood brother; I was my own brother's keeper.

The Struggle To Turn

I knew making a change in my life wouldn't be a bag of chips, so I focused on the things I wanted to accomplish and mapped out the avenues to get there. I knew that I wouldn't get the support of my so-called friends, because if they didn't have a mission they didn't have an ear for yours.

The first step was overcoming the fact that I was living with my father in his one bedroom apartment on the east side of town. I knew he didn't want me there, because he had his own thing going. Even though he wasn't a heavy drinker anymore, he was still a man of the streets. In knowing this, I knew he didn't want any interference.

It's difficult being somewhere and feeling like you're unwanted and being in the way, so I tried to stay out of the way as much as possible. What I did stick around for though was some possible positive conversation. Like son, do you have a plan? Son, it's not too late for college, son which career path do you want to take?

Since that wasn't happening, I would ask myself those questions and answer them the best I knew how. I started by getting up early in the morning going to find the right entry-level professional job. Since I slept on the sofa next to my baskets of clothes, sometimes I wouldn't look the part when I went to fill out applications. I would be wrinkled up and sometimes not very well groomed, so you know that set me apart from the other applicants.

Even though I talked a good game, it didn't matter when it came to some companies. Without prior large company experience, or some type of college education on your resume or application your "AP" was being put at the bottom of the file or in file 13. And I know for a fact once you check the race box on the application, you know, the box next to Black or African American, you're automatically out of the race. I got good after awhile and just out of spite I would check White or leave it blank. That would at least get me an interview. You should've seen the look of disappointment on some of the employer's faces. They were the shortest interviews I ever had.

After long days of job hunting, I would come back to change my clothes if my father was home. I didn't have a key so sometimes I would have to hang around or go other places with my job-hunting gear on. I would go by friend's houses to eat or whatever just to kill time. I always pretended like everything was okay. I was a great pretender at this time.

Mommy would also invite me out to her house to eat and sometimes I would stay overnight. I think she began to feel sorry for me again because I ended up staying with her a couple of nights out of the week. So here I was running around town with a duffle bag staying from one apartment to the next.

My situation frustrated me, but what frustrated me more was the fact that I still didn't know where to start to make things right. All I knew was I had to find a good job. But then I had to ask myself; what is a job without a vision? And without that, I felt like I was almost begging to make a living. "Massa, please can I have a job?"

I know one thing, it's a real bad feeling sleeping on people's couches, keeping your belongings all balled up and hoping I didn't get in anyone's way or make them upset. Not having a single key to a door or a bed to sleep in was horrible and nobody I knew could turn my shoulders in a direction that would be helpful.

To get away from it, sometimes I would stay at friend's houses all night but not too often because I didn't want to wear out my welcome. Sometimes I even slept in abandoned cars or out behind Beatty Recreation Center not far from my father's apartment. That was usually when it got really late and I didn't want to knock on the door to wake him up, or I didn't have bus fare to get out to my moms house. Was this lightweight homelessness or heavy weight?

Sometimes my young brain would ask my heart questions. "Hey bro, why don't you do yourself and everybody else a favor and end this mess!" "Huh, you think they would miss me?" "Yeah, for a week or two then it's back to beans and cornbread for everybody." "Yeah, maybe you're right, I turned out bad, I'm wasted flesh." "How you want to do this Lil' Rommey, here's some broken glass right here, better yet go get the 9mm that you hide from everyone, end your life now!!"

Suddenly, I realized I had two different personalities, one wanted to survive and one wanted suicide. I would talk to myself, and my mental sidekick like a 4 year old talking to an imaginary teddy bear. Feelings of being useless, and unwanted plagued me to the point of having daily visions of death.

As I walked to the abandoned duplex where I hid my 9, tears rolled down my face. I was scared, and my negative mental state was in complete control of my being. Was I mentally ill? Hell yeah I was ill, but guess what, who knew this? I say this to say, watch your actions because your actions can make someone else sick.

As I arrived to my destination of death, I swallowed hard and kneeled down to grab the hidden weapon I had been storing for safe keeping. My hand moved frantically back and forth underneath the porch, but no weapon. Where is it? Did someone see me put it here? It was gone.

A part of me felt relieved, and a part of me felt like I was robbed. But I took it as a sign from my heavenly creator that this sinful act of foolishness won't be allowed in my world. So I cried hard and half-heartedly thanked the Lord and stepped up to the abandoned porch to pray.

"My GOD, why do I feel like this? What's wrong with me? Can you make things right for me? Don't you see I want the best in life? Father, change my life, give me a new job, another new car, I won't mess up anymore. Please GOD please! Amen.

I got off my knees and went to my father's house, and for some reason that few seconds of prayer took all of the energy I had. He let me in and I fell straight to sleep on the couch. I slept until the next morning waking up and full of confidence.

I got dressed and walked to the downtown area to see what job I could find. I tried to look so important with my cheap briefcase in hand. It was black and made of pleather, on real hot day it could melt. In my briefcase I had a couple of resumes and some magazines to make it look full.

I stopped by this temporary agency to fill out an application and to see what was available. Temp agencies were just becoming hot because corporate America found it easier to pay agencies a flat rate without benefits and if they didn't work out, they could end the job assignment.

I filled out the application and sat with a cheesy grin on my face. The receptionist was sexy and gazed over my application with

The Everyday Brother

such grace. I became immediately attracted to her. I glanced at her tanned legs under the open desk and gave her my look of approval that I'd been practicing for so long. She caught the look like Ken Griffey in the outfield and smiled. She sobered up after the immediate thought of what her parents would think if she started having relations with a cute but poor young city boy. "Wait here Rommey, I might have a job for you."

I crossed my fingers and said okay as she walked upstairs to give my AP to a placement coordinator. As she returned to her seat, I mumbled, "If you give me a good job assignment, I'll buy the first meal." "I'm sure you would Mr. Stepney." She replied with a sexy smile.

A tall athletic built white man came downstairs. "Mr. Stepney, come with me please, No let's take the back way." "You know Stepney, these used to be the slave stairs years ago. This is a very old house that has been restored nicely." As I go up the narrow stairway, I thought to myself this MF had to say some stuff like that. This must make him feel like somebody's master.

But anyway, after I let the simple stuff roll off my back, I interviewed with this wannabe master and I just told him how it was. "Look sir, there's an urgent need for me to get into the white-collar workforce starting at ground level working my way up." He stared blankly at me trying not to be impressed with my words. "Okay Mr. Stepney, I have a Mail Clerk position for you at a well known mortgage company. I'll process things for you, get you into orientation so you can start on Monday. Don't disappoint me Mr. Stepney."

After handling all of the paperwork with the sexy Barbie, I went to my father's house to freshen up to go celebrate. But when I got there, things weren't right. His apartment had caught on fire. Being immature and negative, I thought to myself, he set this joint on fire to get rid of me.

"Dad what happened?" "Place caught on fire son, I'm shifting to another unit but in the meantime, take my car to this address and tell me what you think." I took his car to this address and met an older woman there. "Hi, you must be Sunny's boy." "Yes maam." "He said you needed a place to live, so come on in and take a look.

I went in to a one room furnished apartment that was equipped with a bed, TV, table for two, refrigerator, stove, and of course a bathroom. I looked around and imagined myself in here chillin. "It's a start for a handsome young man like you." "It sure is," I said and smiled brightly. "How much?" $150 deposit and $150 a month." "I'll take it!"

It all happened so fast, that I thought I missed something. My first apartment, this is going to be cool. I got my key and receipt, thanked her and moved on. As my father was moving, so was I. Me and my two baskets of clothes.

This would be a new start for me and I appreciated my old man for finding this little bachelor pad for me. He told me once before, "A man needs his own place to live no matter how small it is, one man one set of rules."

Even though I didn't have much, it gave me a sense of self and I was starting to have a little pride. Which meant I wasn't asking anyone for anything unless it was an emergency. You know how it is when you become full of pride.

I equipped my little bachelor pad with a few necessity items that I needed to get by until my cash flow was right. To start, I had purchased plastic forks and spoons, 1 pot, 1 skillet, plastic cups, and a couple of washrags and towels. I used these items like there was nothing left on the planet.

The Everyday Brother

Since I didn't have a car anymore, I walked or caught the bus most places, even to the laundry mat on weekends. It was the same laundry mat that we went to as a kid on Main St. and Champion Ave. It was like I could never get away from where I started.

What really tripped me out was sometimes in my walks to the store or laundry mat, I would see my old homies cruising down the street right pass me. They would see me carrying groceries or my baskets of clothes and keep rolling. I guess since I wasn't riding clean, they had no holler for me. That's cool, I know the definition of a friend and they weren't friends.

I rode the bus to work as well, which didn't bother me as long as I got there. Sometimes, if I ran out of money, I would leave and hour early and just walk. I worked downtown which was about a mile and a half from where I lived.

My temporary job was going well, and I worked very hard to get in full time. I learned the system fast and volunteered for much overtime. Even though I was a mail clerk, I had to wear a shirt and tie and I made sure my attire was nice. I stayed clean cut because corporate America doesn't want to see a black man any other way.

Since my job only consisted of a small amount of blacks, I had to know how white America thought. A lot of people didn't want to work with blacks if they had a choice, and it showed on their faces. Just imagine if there was no Equal Opportunity Employment.

But since I was a hard worker, charming, and developed a great people personality, I got along with most of white corporate well. I was always invited to their outings after hours, and this really gave me a look at what they were really about on the inside.

I noticed that they talked about a lot of things that I couldn't really relate to like, the colleges they went to, the businesses their parents or grandparents own, and a list of other things that I missed out on in my upbringing. So I only chimed in when it came to sports, women, cars, and movies.

My white counterparts talked and ate different from me. I never really paid attention until I came on the same playing field they were on. They held their eating utensils differently, and wiped their mouths during the entire meal. I was used to wiping my mouth after the meal was complete. So you know what I looked like after eating some barbeque ribs or chicken.

At my apartment I practiced talking clearly, trying to get rid of my light stutter that I had. I practiced holding my plastic silverware and using good posture. It was hard for me to get rid of that grip I had on my fork like I was holding a baton in a 400 Meter Relay. But with daily practice, my table manners were more than acceptable.

Since the working class spent a lot of time on the job, you tend to develop relationships with your co-workers. And I developed a lot of relationships with the women. They enjoyed me and I enjoyed them. I still had not grown to discipline myself as far as the physical body and temptation were concerned. The workplace was like a big soap opera, and I was like a broke Victor Newman from The Young and the Restless getting a piece of everybody and having a hold on them.

For some reason I enjoyed this life working to get a paycheck and being a social bumblebee. No, I wasn't a butterfly because I used to bring'em the honey and sting' em.

I was a wanna be businessman during the day the day, and at night depending on my atmosphere I was anything in between a broke gigolo or your average brother from the hood. Whatever I did, I did it well without thinking of the end result of my actions.

I was back into my old ways again, working all day and doing whatever at night. I did a broad range of things including slipping in on college classes in the evenings and on my days off. Sometimes I would take a vacation or sick day and go to the local college and sit in on classes as if I were a paying student.

I did this because I was in denial and still confused, taking below average actions just to make it in the world. I did this to say I went to school, and I only slipped in on the large classes so I wouldn't really be noticed. I also did this to say I went to college but never finished if the conversation came up.

But I learned these classes couldn't prepare me for the real world because I was already in it. Biology, Math, History, and many other subjects could not teach me about respect, love, character, creating wealth, or just being an all out good man. The one book that could take me where I needed to be was the Holy Bible, and the only classes I needed were church and bible study.

Because I had a job, a roof over my head, and something to eat, I was acting like I didn't need GOD on a regular basis. I shouldn't say regular, I should say everyday all day. I was acting like I had no clue as to who was in charge, who gave me life, and who gave me many opportunities.

I was a foolish and selfish young man to only call on my creator when things got really hard for me. I was even more of a fool making the decisions I was making and thinking I wouldn't pay a penalty for my wrong doings and poor choices.

I knew the direction to go, but I just wasn't going. My thought was if I'm not being struck down by lightning, I was okay. So I kept skating on thin ice and displeasing GOD with one thought in my mind. "If I'm alive and breathing, I must be doing okay."

The hot flame that I carried with me would soon be extinguished. I was dating one of my co-workers and we were spending time together on a regular basis. I liked her because she was quiet and to herself, and I could get away with almost anything. I even slept with other women while she waited on the porch for me to finish. I let other women disrespect her by touching on me in front of her.

I used to ask myself, "what's wrong with this woman, is she crazy?" This took my ego to another level, and every time I saw her I gave her the same sly smirk my stepfather gave me. So, I asked her one day, "Baby, why you like me so much, are you sprung on the lovin' like that?" She replied, "No Rommey Stepney Jr. I think I'm pregnant."

When it comes to Rommel Terron Stepney, YOU ARE THE FATHER!!

The System

After hearing this, I go back to that famous knuckle-headed question. "If you are, do you think it's mine?" "Yes, you're the only one I've been with." Notice how that's always said by the young ladies, especially when they know that you're a player. Aw, so only the men play? Yeah well the Maury P. show says different, so I had to ask. He's putting y'all out there now days.

Anyway, this young lady already had a 4-year old son and she didn't need another child. And I knew I wasn't ready, so I had to ask her the other famous question. "You gonna keep it?" "Yes, I think I'm too far along to have an abortion." Yeah okay, whatever. I was foolish thinking the act of abortion was just so easy to do. I recall asking this question so easily to 8 different women.

I was so busy doing my thing that I didn't even recognize the growth in her midsection. My ignorance and arrogance had me thinking she gained a little weight because I was loving her right and she was happy. I smacked myself in the head again as I had visions of being broke with crying babies with a faded wife beater t-shirt on.

I decided to take a week to get my mind in order and work some things out. This meant I had to break my routine of seeing several women that ranged in age from 18 to 50. Since there was no turning back, I took time to laugh, time to cry, and get a plan together. I needed to make a change, and I needed to begin ASAP.

Since I was troubled, I decided to go to GOD with it. I knew my heavenly father was disappointed in me because I only called on him during certain periods in my life. Coming up in church as a youth, I knew the importance of having a relationship with GOD on a daily basis was so important. Since I didn't, it was time to start paying the price.

After talking with the future mother of my child, we decided that we should get a place together. I wanted so badly to do the right thing, because I remember what it felt like not having a consistent father in my life. I wanted to always be there for him/her, to hug, love, advise them, to teach them, to watch them grow. To be the best father I could be.

So we moved in together, still in the hood and not educated enough or financially able to do any better. We lived in a two-bedroom apartment off Main St. on Seymour Ave. We lived right in the middle of crack, violence, and prostitution, so not only would my child be born in sin, he or she would start their growth in sin.

As I planned to better myself so I could pull my new family out of this world, I worked harder and applied for every job promotion possible. During that time, I was very supportive in taking my lady to the doctor and helping out with her son. He had his father in his life, but I still wanted a good relationship with him because I still had a slightly bitter taste in my mouth when thinking about my stepfather.

It was a big adjustment for me because I went from 20 women a week to one. Having the same woman with me every night took some getting used to, and it was like I was a recovering addict or something. I was going through mood swings, not sleeping, not eating, and feeling for the one thing I loved most, having sex with different women.

I held on though, and it gave me a sense of accomplishment that I never felt before. Me being committed to one woman. That was a question I could never ask myself in the past but it was happening. Sometimes I even enjoyed the struggle and would laugh to myself about overcoming difficult times.

Sometimes I even thought of marriage, because I wanted my child to be born into something official and solid.

As I thought of these positive things, there were negative things taking place. My lady wasn't a very clean person domestically, and her son was a very bad hardheaded boy. These are things you don't see when you're just dating.

Coming up, even though I didn't have the best, I was taught to be clean and neat and make the best of what you have. Which meant the house was always clean and my clothes were always clean. I couldn't stand a dirty kitchen and bathroom. I say that to say this; know whom you're getting with completely before making any moves. Not only that, don't just sleep with anyone because there may be a heavy price to pay that you may not like.

Suffering through a lot of unexpected dislikes, I continued to be supportive and take my girl to her doctor's visits. On the last visit though, she went into labor, it was time to bring my seed into the world. As we were escorted upstairs, I noticed that the medical staff was not too personable.

"Are you the husband?" one nurse asked me. "No, I'm the boyfriend, we live together and I've been to every visit with her." "It figures." She said in a mumble. I thought to myself, "Do you know me?" I didn't think so. My second thought was: "Shut the F up and deliver the MF baby, I have benefits so they're covered."

I watched closely as my child was coming into the world. As the nurses did all of the prep work, my girl did all the screaming and dilating, my thought was: after she has this baby, she'll never feel me again. Even in the delivery room, to a degree, I was still thinking about me.

As the head approached, I got real nervous and my stomach turned like a Ferries Wheel. I suddenly felt like the morning after 12 straight doubles of Hennessey and Mickey's Malt Liquor. Those were my drinks that kept me going strong all night long. Yeah, and that's why I'm here, that poison.

After all of this, the doctor finally came in and gave a half-cocked smirk, and never spoke to us as parents. He talked with the nurses, got the numbers, looked at the paperwork, and put on his gear. Even though we were never acknowledged, I thought he was smooth. He inserted his hands through her opening and pulled at the head.

I thought to myself: "Damn, you gonna break the baby's neck!" I bit my lip as I listened to him, "This is a big one ladies, scissors please." "Hey man, what you doin?" I asked. He replied, "She hasn't dilated enough for the shoulders to come through, I have to cut her." He never looked up as he spoke. This offended me. Yeah go ahead and cut up my girl and talk to me with your back turned.

As he cut her all the way to her rectum, I could do nothing but appreciate a woman and what she goes through at birth. I whispered to her; "I love you" as she screamed and made eye contact with me like she hated me. "Here he comes!" the doctor said, as he pulled him out. "Whoa, he's huge!"

"It's a boy," he said in a low tone. As if to say, another black boy in this world. It was like I read his mind or something, but at this point I wasn't concerned. I cried instantly for my child, his mother, and his future. I also cried as a new father, never had a true one, but I was a new one.

The Everyday Brother

"Can I cut the cord doc?" "I'll take care of this one." I knew for a fact husbands get to cut the cord. I got the feeling they were thinking, I was just a boyfriend and my child was another statistic. He cut the cord then carried him to the nurses. Even covered in afterbirth, I knew he was mine. He had the same peanut head, thick eyebrows, and baby muscles. I was still an athlete you know, that's where the muscles came from.

I followed the nurse closely watching her every move making sure nothing went wrong. As she wiped him down, checked him out, and weighed him, I just adored him. I waited patiently for him to open his eyes. I wanted to be sure I was the first person he saw. I wanted him to know daddy was there from day one.

I looked back at his mother as she lay in the bed exhausted and pain stricken. The sweat from the labor had her chocolate skin shining like she just bathed in Armor-All. Her painful look at me said, "You better handle your business." My relieved look at her said, "It's not even about you anymore."

I turned back to the nurse as she said, "10 pounds 5 ounces." "For real?" "Yes for real, do you have a name for him?" "Yes, his name is Rommel Terron Stepney, first name almost like mine, middle name like my best friend Mike C's middle name but spelled different, last name like mine." "You're happy aren't you?" "Yes, are you happy for me?" No response, only a sharp look. Yeah I know this is your job, and the way young people are having babies, job security.

I continued to admire my son and thank GOD for a big healthy baby when suddenly, he opened his eyes. "Hi my son, it's your daddy I'll be with you forever you don't have to be afraid." Maybe it was me, but as I was saying this, his eyes brightened and when I finished, he fell into a deep sleep.

As I thought about my new responsibility, I walked over to his mother and kissed her thanking her for a beautiful son. "You're welcome, that boy is big, it's gonna cost you." She said with a smile. "Hey doc, tie her up, there will be no more after me." I said this with the same smirk I always hated.

My son was my world and I wanted the best for him. Things I never had as a child, I wanted him to have. Since times had changed so did the fashion industry, it wasn't about canvas shoes, it was leather. As a small baby he wore the best and so did his brother. We gave them everything they wanted. But, in reality the things we were giving them had no value they were just material items.

I continued to work hard and do my best to be a good father. Quality time was so important to me, because I remembered my feelings as a child. I never wanted him to feel emptiness, so when I wasn't working, I was trying to be a family man.

It became a little difficult because his mother and I weren't getting along too well these days. She had qualities that I had grown to really dislike, and I had some that she disliked. So this led to me spending more time in the streets again trying to find happiness in a young woman. How could I be happy with someone when I wasn't happy with myself?

I hadn't matured enough yet, so I couldn't answer that question. When times got tough in my relationship, I thought with the wrong head and that would always be my downfall if I let it. In my outings, I would meet women, tell them what they want to hear, cloud their minds with alcohol, and take them home. I didn't mess with you if you didn't have your own place. I did that to make sure I had a place to go if things really got bad at home.

Things did get really bad at times, and I remember when I first got caught up in the system. "If you cared about yourself or anybody else, you would make sure you clean up after yourself!" "Why don't you shut up Rommey?" "Girl, we got kids to raise, you want them growing up like that?" "Well why don't you leave then Mr. Perfect, you're hardly ever here anyway!" "Shut up before I knock you out."

The argument took place in the kitchen just like when I was a little boy. She grabbed a knife and said, "What you gonna do?" I immediately flashed back to when my mother stabbed my father in a fight and it suddenly infuriated me and made my heart ache. "Don't you ever pull a knife on me again, it's not that serious!" I said this as I slammed her into the door to restrain her.

I took the knife from her and threw it in the sink. "Now I'm going to walk away, so don't pick up that knife again. If you do, I'm gonna' have to put you down baby." I had a lot of fighting experience from my days of crooked living, so I wasn't too worried about her. What worried me though, was the two innocent boys watching me. They had the same look of fear in their eyes that I'm sure I had watching my mother and father scrap on a regular basis. Would they blame me? Would they feel the same way I felt? It saddened me that they had to see that. It's time for me to go.

I went upstairs to get dressed, and little did I know she had called to police. I kissed my son and his brother goodbye, and as I walked to the door, to white-shirt police officers met me there. " Is there a problem?" "No sir, no problem here." With their hands on their guns and a racist squint in their eyes, one policeman said: " Oh yes, there's a problem here because we got a call about a domestic dispute."

"Yes, I called y'all, I'm sick of him!" They noticed the look of shock on my face as they made me step further inside like they were looking for a reason to shoot me. "Take the boys upstairs, I don't want them to see this." I commanded. As she made the move to do so, one policeman said: "No, leave them there." He wanted the two growing boys to see this, I hated him for that, and at this point I was ready to risk being shot.

I thought about it though as I let her tell the police her story. Oh yeah, she left out the part about the knife. "What about the knife?" There was silence. "Tell them you pulled a knife on me!" "Shut your face before I shut it for you!" The policeman said. "Hold up dog, don't talk to me like that man." I said calmly. I talked to them calm because I was already in a no-win situation, and after some quick thinking, I didn't want my son to see me get shot.

"That's it, you're going down, take him to the car." "You gonna take him to jail, he has to work tomorrow?" I looked at her as if to say if you called them, they weren't coming for cake and ice cream, they coming to take somebody to jail. As I sat in the car thinking about all of the times I got away with things, I finally got nabbed for some bull.

I sat in the back seat with cuffs on as tight as they could be as they asked me questions and did a warrant check. I looked out the window and she's standing there with my son staring at me. "Take him in the house, he doesn't need to see me like this." She stood there with a look on her face that said to me: Yeah you mess with me, I'll call the white man on you.

As we started for the county jail, I looked at my son with so much disappointment in myself that it made my stomach turn. As I looked at her, she gave me that smirk that I hated most. As if to say, yeah I got you, if you make me mad again, I'll do it all over again. As I bit my lip until it bled, in my mind I changed her title from my lady to my baby's momma, because this was baby mamma's drama.

Upon arriving at the county jailhouse, my stomach began to twist and turn. "I can't believe this is happening to me," I said to myself. Being escorted in handcuffs I felt really low. On the inside, there were plenty of new arrivals waiting to be finger printed and booked. It was a mix of races, some White, Black, and Mexicans. No Chinese or Jewish, because it seemed to me they stuck together to win the battle.

The Everyday Brother

The Jailhouse smelled foul. So foul that if you came in on a full stomach, you might cough up a chunk of what you had to eat. The smell was identical to sweaty armpits and sour feet. You know that armpit smell that resembles old onions, and that feet smell that hit you like old cheese puffs or something.

"Stepney, step up to the red line, strip, and put all money and jewelry in the plastic bag and place it on the counter," said a big man in a sheriff's uniform. He never looked at me, so I knew he had seen it all come through these doors. The pins on his collar told me he was the leader. "Keep your underwear on, this isn't a nudist camp." There was major laughter. "Well, you said strip," I said with a sharp tone. "Don't get smart with me son, because if you were smart, you wouldn't be in my jailhouse!" I silently agreed with him.

I was placed in a holding tank with several other men, we looked like defected cattle waiting to be slaughtered and burned. Some were drunk, some were bloody, and some looked tired from being on the run. There was a sink and a toilet in the open, which meant if you had any business to take care of, everyone would be in your business.

What saddened me though, were the black men who acted like it was the in thing to be there. They compared their misdemeanors and felonies like there would be a trophy at the end of the day. They talked about whom they robbed, whom they beat, and their earnings behind it all. "Hey cuz, whatcha in here fo?" One brother asked me. "Not what you in here fo," I said mockingly. "Man this ain't nothing to be proud of," I continued. "Hey cuz, you can save that for when you get out, because right nenh, you in heeya wit me." Once again I had to silently agree.

After 4 hours in the holding tank, I was escorted to a cell that held 8 to 10 people. Or should I say inmates, animals, better yet, I'll say fools because that's what we were. I saw men I hadn't seen in a while, and some familiar faces that I had seen before in the streets, like at nightclubs or parties.

I was really surprised at how many men were locked up in the county jail. We were all crammed together from different backgrounds. Black, white, mama's boys, orphans, whatever we were all there. In here, we were all the same. We all committed some kind of crime, we all failed as men at some point.

As I continued to scope my environment, I unrolled my smelly plastic mattress, spread my worn out sheet over it, and covered that with that wooly blanket they give you and tried to make as neat a bed as possible.

The old faces that I knew tried to spark conversation, but I wasn't in the mood for it. I just wanted to lay down and clear my head. That evening, I had time to think about so many things, my life, my son's life, and just moving on. My mind became so heavy I had no choice but to fall into a deep sleep.

"Breakfast, get up, trays up!" One of the working inmates yelled. "Who don't want they breakfast, give it to me," one of my cellmates yelled. "Hey Rome-Rome, you want your grub man?" "I sure do," I said with a hoarse voice and morning breath.

I slipped on my worn out plastic slippers and stepped in line. I looked at my arms and rubbed my face only to see and feel I had a major rash. I just shook my head and wondered how many different feet had been in these plastic slip-ons.

I grabbed my tray, which consisted of a cereal box, 1milk, 1 donut, and some orange drink that was poured in the cup that they give you along with your bedding and toothbrush. It reminded me of free lunch days back in school. The only difference was the drink had no sugar, and the donut had the texture of French Bread.

After a tasteless breakfast, the county deputy called out a list of names to prepare for morning court. My name was one of them. "Be ready in twenty minutes," he said. I went to take a shower to freshen up and look halfway decent. The shower smelled like someone pissed in it. But what I didn't know was shower or not, I still look the same with the county blues on.

We were escorted to court through hallways and tunnels only to get more sets of bars in our face. Then we were lined up like fifth graders to wait our turn to see the judge. It really tripped me out how so many people made so many mistakes on the same day around the same time. It explained why we were rushed through like pop cans at a soda factory.

I didn't have a lawyer to call, so I was met by a Public Defender. He gave me a short story on what the police wrote on their report. "Mr. Stepney, you are being charged with domestic violence with assault." I looked him up from the top of his oily head down to his plastic run down shoes. "What! Man I didn't assault anybody!" "It sounds worse than it really is, but we can get the assault charge dismissed."

"Why don't I just speak for myself, because you want me to admit to something that's not true?" "Well, thing is Mr. Stepney, it's my job to talk to the judge for you, that's what lawyers are for." "So you saying I can't talk to the judge and tell him my side of the story?" "Truth is Mr. Stepney, the judge doesn't want to hear your side. Again, that's why I'm here to tell your side."

I had heard stories about the justice system, but I witnessed it first hand. When my time came to stand in front of the judge, he looked at me with this disgusted look then turned away never to look up at me again.

My baby's momma was there surrounded by a group of white women from this battered women's group or something giving her false support. Did they know me? Did they know her? Have you ever been in a struggling black family? I didn't think so, so back up.

I was hit with a domestic violence charge and a boatload of humiliation. As I was escorted out, the public defender said, "Don't be upset Mr. Stepney, you're in the system now and this is how it works, see you next time." He said this with a sarcastic smile like he knew I would be back. But you know what? He was right.

After getting out of the grip of the county for the last two days, I had a lot of time to think about what I needed to do next to get out of a dead end, unhappy situation. My only concern though was my son, and how he would react to daddy's leaving. He was too young to understand that it wasn't him, and I didn't want him to feel like I felt coming up. I didn't want him to feel like he was a part-time job.

"Listen, we're not getting along, and we want two different things out of life. I want something and you just want to get by. So, I think I'm going to find me a place to live on my own, but I want my son to live with me." "No, that's not going to happen," she said. "You can see him anytime you want."

I agreed to this, but little did I know it would not be that easy. "Okay, and I'll continue doing the things that I do, like buying his shoes and stuff, haircuts, quality time, and whatever else. Oh, and if his brother wants to come too, he's more than welcome, cuz you know I got love for him. But just check with his dad too though, cuz I don't want no drama." "That's fine," she said. "Just give me 30 days," I said.

After telling one of my close partners of my plan, He suggested that we become roommates for a while, because he was in search of a new place himself. He was in a relationship that had gone sour as well. So, after work each day we would go apartment hunting until we found the right spot to set up shop and save some money.

After searching for a short period, we found a nice apartment on the north side of town with a pool right next to the front door. This was nice, and all we could think about was becoming the ultimate bachelors, taking girls swimming late at night in the nude. See, I was only ready to change my environment and not my way of thinking.

So I moved out to my new apartment happy about starting over, but leaving things behind so I would have a reason to come back and do things, if you know what I mean. You see, at the time I was so selfish to the point where she wasn't good enough for me, but nobody else could have her. I was her baby's daddy and I wanted control.

After my partner and I settled in, we ran the streets and moved women through the place like the New York subway system. We continued to work hard, because we believed in becoming successful one day, but for right now, we were still at war with our physical bodies. He was in college, and I admired that in him. Since I had basically stolen some college education in the past, I felt like I didn't need it anymore. Plus, my honest opinion at the time was, college wouldn't prepare me for what I go up against in this world. I felt that additional education made you a first choice in corporate America.

I say this because from elementary all the way through high school I learned things that never pertained to my culture or me. Martin Luther King was brought up every now and then, Rosa Parks, and Malcolm X. But I needed more than just the march in the streets, Rosa Parks taking a front seat, and Malcolm X's saying: "By any means necessary." They made it all sound so simple and it really wasn't. But that was my one track mind, because I could've easily went to a historical black college and got more. Do you see where I'm going with this, or do you see where I just went? It was about choices.

But anyway, I was having so much fun and working too hard to see that I had mail on the counter from almost a week ago. "What's this, Child Support Enforcement? I wonder what they want," I said. I opened it up to see my son's name on the paperwork. I had a meeting to establish child support! Oh, here we go again, first the county jail now child support! I was getting caught in the system in more ways than one.

"Hey what's up? I got this letter from child support talkin' bout a meeting to establish child support, you know anything about that?" "Yes I do Mr. Man. I need to make sure we get our money while you out there with all these other women. We want ours first!" she yelled. "Don't I take care of my son?" I asked her. "Yeah, but just in case you don't see him, I know I'll still be able to provide for him." Yeah okay now you want to call all the shots, you trying to be slick.

The child support office was in the same building as the county jail. So you know they were tied in together. "Oh I see, if you don't pay your child support your butt is going right next door," I thought. In this area it seemed to be a lot of tension, and I fit right in.

Just like the jail, we were rushed in and out like there wasn't much time left on this earth. My son's mom acted like she didn't even know me, even though we were still having physical communication from time to time. "Oh I see, when you got the white man on your side, you get brand new," I said.

When it was time to see the child support officer, I took a deep breath and walked in. The support officer never looked up at me, and only made eye contact with my son's mom. The people on the other side of the system felt they were better than the people they dealt with. I pleaded my case by saying: "I've always been here for my son, so I don't even know why I'm here." She gave that smirk I grew up to hate then said: "Proof of income please," never looking at me.

This whole situation frustrated me because first of all she already had a child, one whom you never sought child support for, two, I was already a father to my son, but you got me downtown looking like a deadbeat. Now I had to catch on to the game plan of a single deadbeat mother.

The Everyday Brother

To me, the game plan went like this: Okay, this young brother is a struggling young man. He's trying hard to be something to his son that he's never had, I see potential in him that he doesn't see in himself. Someday, he might get his program right and when he does, I have to make sure my hand is in his pocket. To me, this is the thought of the single deadbeat mother. House the child and get all the credit.

It seems that the single black female got to the psychological side of the judicial system before the young black man could even get a clue. Now a new enemy has joined forces with America, and it's a black woman who uses the system against you when there's no need to.

It goes like this: If you make me mad, I'll sic the system on you and it will add a lot of extra weight to your struggle. I will continue to be on your mind, and when you get your paycheck, you will feel what I'm capable of. I'm mad at you, so I will show you that every step you make with the right foot, there will be quicksand at the left foot.

Furthermore, I will keep my own personal record of your employment history, your raises and promotions, and your social security number. If you get married or have a good relationship with someone else, I will file for a child support increase, because I want some of hers too. I am apart of your every struggle and accomplishment. And yes, I will use the money to buy high-dollar purses and shoes, leaving you to pay child support plus pay for his haircuts, shoes, and everything else. This is just a part of their anthem.

My response to this is, I should've been selective and waited until marriage before I started laying it down with just anyone. I should've really gotten to know someone before putting my life at risk in so many different ways. I now have to pay the price for not valuing myself, and dealing with people of no value. So what are you mad at me for? I'm just an everyday brother trying to make it happen. So who are you mad at for real, you, or me?

If this doesn't pertain to you, keep reading. If this does pertain to you keep reading, and get to know a brother and where he comes from. I'm not talking about what city, I talking about where he comes from on the inside. Are you there to love and support him, or are you there because you like what he does, where he works, what he drives or how he does it?

There is no more room for temporary assignments, there's no more temp to hire. At some point, all positions should be permanent positions with extensive background checks. To me, everything was based on how I felt at the moment, and I learned that sometimes a few minutes of pleasure could lead to years of headache and heartache. Please turn the page after the beep. Beep.

The Breaking Point

As time and life moved on, I continued to work and play, and my time was being shortened as far as being a young father was concerned. Sometimes, it was hard to catch up with my son, and I know that was the intentional plan. I could sense that my baby's momma would purposely disappear with him so I couldn't see him. She knew how important it was to me to be there for my son, but this was a tactic to really get under my skin.

I channeled my frustrations by using other women to make me feel better. This was only a temporary fix, and sex only made things better for the moment. I also became a very heavy drinker to drown out how I was feeling emotionally, but this only added to the problem, it made me have violent streaks.

As I struggled with my emotions and having many different faces and lives, it made life more confusing and added very little progress in achieving the many different goals I had in mind. When I looked in the mirror, I only saw what I hated as a child, and I hated myself for having a good heart but an unstable body and mind.

Work continued to be good for me though, because I learned the corporate game through having different jobs and a lot of reading. In my spare time, I interacted with people I had no business interacting with, but because my mind was like an octagon with many sides, I felt it was necessary to be in many different worlds until I was certain of where it was I wanted to go.

But one of my favorite places to go was Club Alexander's, which was on the east side in the neighborhood where I grew up on Main St. Alexander's was open all week long, but my favorite nights were Monday, which was dollar Michelob Night, Stripper Night, and Friday Night Happy Hour because they had good food.

I was a regular customer, so I got a lot of drink specials from the bar staff and my treatment was royal. I frequented many other spots, but Al's was my favorite. It was also a meat market for a street man like me who was somewhat well known. I had no problems with closing the bar down on any of these nights.

I wanted so badly to get out of this world, but still through the years I couldn't get out of this tight web. I liked the nightlife, and for some reason this just eased my mind of my shortcomings. I still lived from day to day and my life's resume showed it by the way I would just up and leave jobs and women. I still hated my inner self. But, it was over shadowed by loud music and pretty women. I loved my physical being because I was decent-looking, well versed, and had a way with women. This was the only way I could tolerate myself.

I was also playing semi-pro football at the time, and I guess I was trying to relive the past. I was still a good athlete, and I felt that I shouldn't totally waste it. This was also my way of saying: "I'm a bad guy, but I'm a good guy too. I took out a lot of frustration on the field. I was a Defensive Back and a very hard hitter.

It was something how a man in his prime can do so many things; work all day, play football, basketball and run track. Then see plenty of different women all week. I thought I was doing something, but all I was doing was wasting my time and everyone else's. And once again, as long as I was eating, sexing, and having fun, I had no time for my heavenly creator.

If I was in my true prime, I would've been working, saving my money and my body, been involved in a relationship with GOD and talking to him every hour of the day, and also thinking of a plan to create wealth. But, I wasn't into that I was too caught up in keeping up with the world and things of the world.

You know, I thought I was something keeping up with the latest tennis shoes and outfits, but all I was doing was trying to give the world what I thought they wanted to see. If I were smart I wouldn't have been living for the world, I would've been living for me.

One weekend after a semi-pro game, my dude Jamo and I decided to go to Al's for a few drinks and to celebrate a tough win. We always met the rest of our crew there, just in case something jumped off and we needed immediate response. This night was somewhat different because I wanted to meet someone special also I was tired of all the drama.

I evaluated myself and my progress that evening, and I asked myself what it was I wanted to accomplish in life. Since I had been through many jobs and had experience in different areas, I needed to put that experience to good use, and if I wanted to be with someone, they had to be in my corner.

I was the kind of person who wanted to be with someone, but I was tired of being with the same type of woman who already had kids and drama in their life. I couldn't really be picky at this time, because I had a child myself, but the drama was over. So maybe I could tolerate someone else's child as long as there was no drama.

But anyway, while we were out that night I changed my game plan. I didn't dance much, and I kind of just stood in one spot saying my player type hellos and my what's' ups from where I stood. I still drank a lot though, that wasn't going to change in me just yet. I guess I just wanted to get a good look at what I've been doing and whom I've been doing all this time, wasting my time.

Let me rewind for a minute and tell you about my boy Jamo. Jamo, who's real name is James, is my partner I met while playing football. When I was between jobs and didn't have a ride, he was there for me. He understood my pain and I understood his. So we became close and if we weren't with a woman, we were together. He always told me; " Rome you my nigga til' death due us part, until death due us part nigga, do you hear me nigga?" Then he would give me a head butt.

He was a soldier who served in the Saudi Desert, and I thought he was a little touched at times. But come to find out, he was just a modern day Black Panther. Sometimes I wouldn't catch on to some things he said until four days later, that's just how deep he was.

Any hoo, a group of young ladies came in the club that looked good, but they were conservative. They spoke to my boy Jamo as if they knew him. "Hey Jamo, who dem' girls you just hollered at?" "Aw, they just some girls I know from school and church." "Aw, so you holdin out on your boy?" "Nah Rommey Rome, I'll introduce you."

One of the young ladies really caught my eye, she was yellow, average looking but pretty, and her skin was smooth and soft looking. "Hey Jamo, who's the yellow bow-legged one?" Aw, that's T, I used to go to church with her, her father's a preacher." "Aw, that's just what I need, a preachers' daughter to give me a boost to get my life in order," I said. But then I thought to myself, how much boost can she give me, if she's out here where I am?

The Everyday Brother

I was introduced, and she seemed a little dry. Yeah that's cool I thought, but I wanted to meet someone who wasn't half dressed and didn't have the tone of drama in her voice. So I was patient and convinced myself that I would like to get to know her. I noticed she knew a lot of guys, and like UTFO used to say; "I hate the girl who knows every guy, before you introduce her, she already says hi." You cold wanna be wit me because……… remember that?

She was in the club every weekend just like me, so I started to wonder how much religion was in her. I saw her leave a couple of times with guys but I thought maybe she just wanted to leave early because her girls were still there. Even though I wasn't the only dog that existed, I still gave her the benefit of the doubt.

One weekend, I told her I wanted to be with her all night and every dance belonged to me. She accepted and we danced and talked the night away. Some of the other women in the club didn't like my new attitude, but I pulled them aside and told them not to mess with her. These women were used to me sexin them up after the club from time to time, but all that had stopped because I liked this young lady.

"Rome, why you all on her like that, she don't like you, plus I heard she still wit her baby's daddy." "Aw she got a kid?" I asked. "Hell yeah, and she handicapped too!" My little skeezer said. "Listen hear ho, if you mess with her, I'm goin' cut you!" I told her. "And you know I will, so don't play wit me."

I walked over to this young lady I was so interested in and asked her if she wanted to go to Denny's after the club. She accepted. My plan was to talk with her over breakfast and see if my new findings about her personal life were true. Normally, my partners and I would take girls to Denny's to fatten them up for the kill if you know what I mean.

The selfish side to me wanted to be upset, but the realistic side said, "look man you got more skeletons than the Greenlawn Cemetery, so don't get funny." Not only that, I was living with a woman on part-time basis, and still messing around with my son's mom from time to time. So was I really in the position to question anyone about their life when my own back yard was dirty?

So we went to Denny's and ate never really speaking on our past or present lives, and my objective was just to get a little closer to her. For some reason I wanted her to give me what no other young woman could give me. Why I chose this woman I wasn't sure, but I had yet to learn if I wanted to change what I was getting, I needed to change my atmosphere. Also, I had not yet learned a good woman will come to you. You don't have to chase and choose. Do you see where I'm going with this?

To make a long story short, yes, I'm going to make this short because too many words might make her think I'm all on her, she thinks like that. But, since this is my life and she was in it, I have to give her a few words. Anyway, we started dating and seeing each other on more than a regular basis.

I was trying to end the other relationships I had because I really wanted to do better and to have better. I was still walking that thin line between jobless and homeless, and love and hate. Starting over was really harder than I thought, especially if you don't start over with GOD first. So I was confronted with more drama and struggle.

Also, by this time I had made a few more visits to the Franklin County Jail, and it seemed like those nasty slippers I hated so much became my own personal pair. It was almost like the sheriff's were saying: "Put those in the corner for Rommey Rome, he'll be back in a couple of months." And I could almost swear the blanket I had the last visit smelled like the cologne that I had on the visit before. Maybe it was my mind telling me I been there too much.

What also tripped me out was on each return visit to the county, I seen some of the same faces that I had seen in the past. It just went to show me that I wasn't the only one making bad choices and hanging in the wrong places, dealing with the wrong people. In a strange way, this made me feel comfortable seeing the same people making the same mistakes. But it should've saddened me.

I also went through a lot of career changes because of my uncertainty of who I was and what I wanted. All I wanted to do was free myself of my past and to live like a young man in his right mind and spirit should live. So I did what most of us do, go to GOD expecting a sudden change.

So here I am going back to different churches trying to see which one I was going to join, trying to get right with GOD. I would always sing the song: Get right with GOD and do it now, get right with GOD and he will show you how. That was my church song, and if you sing it in devotion with some passion, I was known to shed a few tears.

So hear I was trying to get right with GOD and still dating this young lady T. We had a good relationship and we concentrated on spoiling each other. I had met her daughter whom I loved like my own child. She has Cerebral Palsy, which is to my knowledge a permanent disability. But if I wanted to be with her, I was willing to accept the total package. And I didn't just love her child I cared for her as well.

So here we are one day preparing to go to a movie and she says, "Rome after the movie, I need to talk to you about something." Here I was throughout the whole movie thinking, "maybe she wants to take things to the next level or something." But in the middle of the movie it hit me. "Damn, I hope she ain't pregnant," I whispered to myself. "Did you say something Rome?" "No, I was talking to myself, just enjoy the movie baby," I responded.

After a good movie, I was certain of what our little talk would be about. I was good to her, and had been somewhat of a faithful man, so it had to be what I feared most. "Rome, I haven't had my period yet, I think I'm pregnant." I knew it. "Well what you wanna do?" I asked her, "We already got 1 kid a piece," I said like I was talking of two objects. "Let's just hope my cycle is changing," she said. Then I had my silent thought, "If she is, I wonder if it's mine."

Well as it turned out, yes, she was pregnant, and here I was again unprotected and unmarried. I had taken the same risk over and over again, and the end result was pregnancy. I chose to ignore the fact that if I wasn't ready for another child, why was I having unprotected sex? Why was she having unprotected sex? It takes two, and both of us were irresponsible.

Then here I was again beating myself up after the fact, when I should've been beating myself up before the act. Then I asked myself, could we really afford to take care of this child on our incomes with two other children between us? Who would the baby live with? I had a roommate and she still lived at home with her parents. What is her father, who is a good minister thinking of our character and our actions?

Well, I knew one thing. The job I had at the time was a stock and cashier clerk at a local liquor store. And at $5.50 an hour, one more child on my salary would put me on death row financially. Between paying my part of the rent and child support, I was already in a financial straightjacket. Yes I said straightjacket because them child support people will make you a mental case. They gonna get theirs no matter how much you make.

I had already been looking for a better job, a company I could grow with, so it was just a matter of time before something came through. In the meantime though, I knew another child would be born and I had to get ready. I made that promise to myself, no matter how many children I have I will be there for them.

The stress of a part-time salary and the birth of a new baby coming soon really started getting to me. Once again, I was being shot down by a lot of companies finding an entry-level position. My so-called friends always said the companies they worked for were never hiring, but it was funny their companies would have ads in the Sunday paper.

One day, a group of my friends were at one of my partners house for a little get together when I yelled out, "Hey fellas, I need a better paying job with benefits, so give me a shout if you hear of something." There was silence in the room. This was one thing that really pissed me off. I'm good enough to kick it with, but not good enough for a job reference.

As the stomach on my girlfriend continued to grow, I felt more discomfort every time I saw her. And once again, I saw myself scraping up change for a pack of Huggies in a dirty wife beater t-shirt. Even though she worked and was a spoiled child, I felt I should bear most of the responsibility as a father.

For some reason, what I feared most was not being a good father to my children. And even if I wasn't always around, I could provide for them. Was this because I was somewhat fatherless as a child? Was it because of the craving I had for a role model left me empty? I'm sure it had something to do with it.

The pressure had come to a boil and I had to do something. So I called one of my partners and I tell him of my situation and how I needed more money. He says: "Dog, I know of a way to put some extra cheese in your pocket until you get that job you're looking for." "For real, what I gotta do?" I asked. "Man it ain't legal but, you can stack some chips."

I accepted my good friends offer and I met with him to discuss all of the particulars and his group of contacts. My need for an increase in finances clouded my judgement, and once again here I was being impatient and foolish. Instead of me having faith that everything would be okay, I had to try to do things my way.

I made excuses for my actions, and my denial of the fact that these actions were wrong and would place me in the land of ruins. All I could say was; "$200.00 every two weeks just ain't happening, I need some more money." I used this excuse for my actions along with many others.

So here I was hustling in preparation for a new child, I worked during the day, and hustled on evenings and weekends. Things were going good and I was stacking a few chips for baby clothes and things of that nature. I felt good about my little hustle because I wasn't doing it for a nice ride or anything, I was doing it for the children.

I didn't say much about it to my girl, but I'm sure she had it figured out because of all the late hours that I kept. All she would say was; "Rome be careful." I would just take those words and smile because for some strange reason I thought I was unstoppable and untouchable.

One afternoon I get a call from my girl and she told me her water broke and it was time to have the baby. I arrived at the hospital scared, nervous, and happy which led to an upset stomach. Here I was in the same situation as before just in a different hospital, having another baby by a single mother who already has a baby.

"Are you the hubby?" One nurse asked as she smiled. "No I'm the boyfriend," I replied. Her smile instantly turned cold as she sharply said; "follow me." I felt her facial expression cast judgement on me, as I wanted badly to plead my case. But that wouldn't do any good. She was like many other people who had their minds made up about a young black man.

After being totally ignored as a new father, I felt I still had a role in this baby coming into the world. "Is there something I can do until she's fully dilated?" I asked. "Sure, be a helpful dad and hold this pan up to her mouth, she's feeling sick," One nurse said. "That's being a helpful dad," she said sarcastically.

After a few moments of intense labor, it was time for my baby to come into the world. "Here comes the head!" The doctor said. The head had that unique peanut shape that I couldn't deny, just like that of my son. And here she is, it's a girl! I was speechless as I looked at the exhausted face of the mother.

"Can I cut the cord doc?" I asked. "I'll take care of it," he said never looking up. I accepted that because I had been turned down before, and I could only accept stories of fathers who cut their babies cords. So I swallowed the rejection and followed the nurses to watch my daughter get cleaned up and weighed. Before I left, I kissed my girl and thanked her for a lovely little girl. "Baby you okay? Thank you for my daughter, I love you." Had I been here before? Hell yes.

Imani was the name that we chose for her, and I felt proud to have named both of my children. She was a beautiful tiny little being with a smile like that of her father. I made my second promise to do what ever I could for her even if it meant giving my life for the lives of my children. Even if it meant breaking the law so they could eat.

Imani's family on her mother's side was a loving family, and I didn't have to break any laws to feed her. What we didn't do, her grandparents did, my mother included. I just chose to continue doing my hustle because that's what I wanted. I still wanted more money because the hustle was available.

But things were looking up too, because I just got a job I was trying to get at this manufacturing plant that made nutritional formulas and baby milk. I started off as a temporary and got hired on full-time in no time. Which was cool because it was one of the better paying companies in the city, especially without having a college degree.

I decided since I had this good job, there would be no reason for me to continue my illegal hustle, so I told my partner I just needed one big hit this weekend and I was done. I had a funny feeling about the weekend though, like I knew something was going to happen and the end result would not be good.

The weekend came with a flash, and I was caught up in the web of a working man, a family man and part-time hustler. Something didn't feel right about the arrangement my partner had made to make a move in a white club on the mostly white side of town.

"Hey man, let's do what we gotta do and get the hell outta here," I said nervously. In an instant, my mind suddenly thought of the time I could be spending with my children. While thinking warm fatherly thoughts, I looked up to see my partner being rushed to the back of the building by three white men.

I went to make a move in their direction to rescue him but, I was stopped by two more white men with guns. "Sir, you don't want to do that, keep your hands where I can see them and walk slowly to the back," one man said. "Who the F are you?" I asked. "We're the Secret Service," he said with a look that could cut through train wheels. "This is just great!" I said with a whisper.

It seems that the secret service got a tip that we would be there, or maybe it was just meant to be for us to get busted. The secret service confiscated our illegal goods and told us to report to their office on Monday morning. "If you don't come on your own, we will come for you, and it won't be good," one agent said.

Since I didn't want them coming to my job, I put it on my calendar for the first thing Monday morning. Since I was on night shift, I didn't have to miss work, nor did I have to let them in my business. I knew there would be a price to pay, because I was on probation, and probation means keep your butt out of trouble.

I continued to beat myself up, and all I had to do was make the right decisions. It wasn't hard to do, it was just identifying right from wrong and not taking any action on the wrong end. It seemed to me the only reason I was on both sides of the fence was because I wanted to be accepted by everyone, so that meant being a good person around good people, and a bad person around people who only want the worst out of life.

"Heavenly father, please forgive me for all the wrong I've done, please carry me through this. I promise I'll be a better man Lord please don't let me go to prison." Once again, I was only going to GOD when I was in trouble, and I think GOD was probably mad at me for being so selfish. I was using GOD and I would have to suffer.

Even though things were going good with my children, my relationship, and my job, something was still eating away at me. The pressure of an upcoming court date, and my unhappiness from within gave me more discomfort than a priest in a whorehouse. I knew I was a better person than what I displayed, and it became very hard to deal with.

To deal with the pain, I started blaming everyone from my childhood again. I blamed both of my so-called fathers, I blamed my mothers no-good boyfriends, and I blamed my mother. I wanted someone to blame because I couldn't be a man and own up to my own responsibilities. Even though I was a so-called man, I had childish blame.

During my inner struggles, I continued to work hard and be the best father I could be. I had a couple of promotions and things were looking good. I had developed more of a relationship with GOD, so my struggle lightened a little, and I focused more on setting goals.

I got a little house on the north side of town, and it gave me a sense of accomplishment like never before. My girlfriend's father was an awesome preacher who spoke from and lived from the Holy Bible, and we developed a relationship as well. Her family made me feel like I was their family and I felt like I belonged.

My court date was coming up soon, and I knew I was being watched by the secret service. I could tell by the clicks on the telephone, and the strange white men in the neighborhood. It didn't bother me though, because my focus was to be the best man I could be. I had children who were counting on me, and a woman who loved me. Not only that JESUS loved me, he died for my sins.

My court date just so happened to be on my birthday, how ironic they set that up on my birthday. "They want to lock me up on my birthday!" I said. I didn't seem too worried though. I just wanted it to be over with, no matter the outcome, I knew I had to pay the price. My girlfriend and my mother came to the hearing to show support, I appreciated it, but I was thinking they didn't know if they would see me for a while.

In court, they chopped me up like deli turkey breast. They talked about my grades in school, where I grew up, and what my family was about. To me, the courts tried to make me look like a no-good black man who never been anywhere and wasn't going anywhere. They even did character interviews with family and friends to tell them what kind of person I was. Afterwards, my attorney told me, "Well Rommey, if it was left up to your mother's opinion of you if you lived or died, you would be dead." That crushed me beyond words.

Anyway, I got off with just house arrest and probation, which meant I had to wear this beeper-like thing around my leg. I was only allowed out of the house during work hours and for travel time. They did give me time out for church on Sunday, but I had to fight for that. What was that about? You don't want me to serve GOD?

It was difficult trying to hide this, because sometime I had to work overtime, and if you're going to be late, you have to call your probation officer. I sometimes would get teased by my co-workers; "You checking in Rommey Rome, I thought you wore the pants?" They would joke. My thought was; "Man think what you want, I'm checking in to prevent lockup!"

I promised myself after my three months house arrest, I would get married, and boy was that the longest three months of my life! I held on strong though and made it through with out any issues. Now my plan would be to get into a bigger home, because the home I was in was a two bedroom. I had to have room for my son, daughter, and stepdaughter.

That Christmas, I presented my girlfriend with a ring of engagement by way of her fathers approval. Immediately after, she started planning, and we set a date for September 25, 1999. "Rommey you know I never really liked you when I met you, I had to grow to like you, look at us now," she said. Wow, that cut like a knife, and there was an imbalance in our feelings from day one.

On the job, I was still doing well, and received a couple more promotions and I felt really good about myself. My other half focused mostly on planning the wedding, and she put more time into that than she did into me. I would've been happy with something small and simple, but you know how some people have to go and break the bank just to please everyone else.

As time moved on, I started to feel a little uncomfortable as I noticed a change in her attitude. It was like she wanted to be in total control of everything, and all I was supposed to do was shut up and work. We hadn't lived together yet, so I was thinking maybe it was the stress of planning a wedding.

After months of planning and a few thousand dollars, it was time to officially tie the knot. The wedding was beautiful, and the honeymoon to St. Thomas was special. I was drained from hard work and stress, and I just wanted to relax. I enjoyed the blue ocean water and all of the eating, spending, and sightseeing.

As the honeymoon was coming to an end, I thought; what would it be like at home now? What would it be like with a wife at home? Even though I questioned it, I looked forward to being a husband, and I made a second promise to give someone what I wanted my own mother to have. A good husband is what every grown woman needs, I thought to myself as my intent was to be one. But does every woman deserve one?

I knew we all had to make a new adjustment, my wife and kids coming from her parent's house, and me living with a woman and children again. I had been in the situation before, a woman, our child, and another mans' child, so I somewhat knew how to deal with things, and what to expect.

One of the things I didn't expect was the mailman bringing me another letter from children support. "What's this?" I thought, I'm already good with child support, so why are they sending me stuff in the mail? But guess what it was? Brothers, I know you know, and you know I know you know.

Yeah, you guessed it. It was a support increase letter at the request of my son's mother. You know every couple of years, child support can do a review for increase in support, and it didn't surprise me that my son's mother would know all the laws of child support.

You know what trips me out, is so many women can know all the laws of support and income, but don't know how to keep a man or make their own money. So what do they do? They keep up with your income, and live their lives off your income.

"Hey what's up woman?" I asked, "I just got this letter from child support talkin' bout an increase or something." "You know what that is Rommey Rome, you went off and got married, so your income doubled, and I know she work in the State Building." She said. "That should've been me!" She added.

"What you mad at me for?" I asked, "My son is well taken care of, plus I put money in his pocket when he's wit' me!"

I shared this information with my new wife, and this infuriated her, so much to a point where it seemed like she had a dislike for my son. Even though she didn't outright say it, but I know a fake smile when I see one. "Why didn't you fix his plate, you fixed everyone else's?" I asked one day. "Rome, I don't know what he likes, so don't yell at me!" She said. "He likes what you just cooked, you've known him for four years, now you don't know what he likes? Don't play me!" I added sharply. See, it was stuff like that that heated me. Already, damn!

I trusted and depended on my new wife to be there for me and to understand me. I trusted her with my innermost feelings and hurts from my childhood to adulthood. So to me, that meant you should be feeling me at this point, understanding my pains and desires. But she was on a different page. Soon she would become another female opponent.

"Hey baby, my child support has increased a little, so can you pay the utility bills, you know, gas, phone, and electric?" I asked. "Well Rome, I ain't used to paying no bills, and I ain't gonna start," She added. "Well, if you can't help out, ain't no need for you to be here," I said.

Needless to say, we only got along on occasions and I spent more time enjoying myself with the children than I did being a husband. Not saying that's bad, but at least I had some good times. It was difficult for me to enjoy her when if something didn't go her way, she would use everything I told her against me.

"How do you know how to be a man, when you never had a real father in your life? What do you know about marriage, your mother wasn't married long? I hate you with a GOD given passion." These were some of the statements that took away my confidence, and chipped away at my manhood.

In less than a year, my marriage was sour, and my work performance on the job was fading away. Before I knew it, I had silent thoughts of suicide, and management had recommended me for counseling before I reached the point of job jeopardy.

"Hey baby, I thought about going to counseling and I would like for you to go, it would be good for our marriage." I mentioned. "What do I need counseling for, my father is a preacher," she added. So I went to counseling on my own never bothering her about it again. I was wrong to think someone with a religious upbringing had religion and support in them. I had realized that was just her family.

Summer days at home felt like winter, because there was hardly any conversation, and I didn't even feel like the man of the house. So, I tried to stay away as much as possible, so after work I would go to the bar and sulk like all the rest of the unhappily married men in town. I tried to get home when I thought she would be in bed, only to kiss the kids good night and sometimes sleep on the sofa or fall asleep in the car in the driveway.

This wore me down and I think she enjoyed every minute of it. It really hurt me that someone would want to see me fail, someone who I committed myself to, and someone I trusted with my heart, my manhood, and my life. This created a wall that could not be broken down.

My unhappiness led to many drunken nights and extra-marital affairs, which caused more problems. I drifted away from the church I had joined because I felt so ashamed. Should I be ashamed when I gave my best? Well I was, because I wanted something I never grew up with, so here I was beating myself up again.

Once again, I strayed away from my creator who made it all happen and I was trying to do it all on my own again. Well, doing it on my own got my in trouble with the law again. I was arrested for DUI after a long night of depressed drinking, which got me back in them same old plastic slippers and blue jump suit. I still hadn't learned about letting other peoples actions affect my decisions.

Not only that, I had domestic problems at home and the police were called to my house on one occasion. And here I was going back to the county. I was still messing with folks I had no business messing with, and then I'd be the one getting in trouble. Back to the county blue, and still didn't have a clue.

This time, I was ordered by the court to take Domestic Violence and Anger Management courses. Here I was in a class with a bunch of men talking to a group leader who had a silver spoon in his mouth as a child telling me what I should do in a drama situation. "Have you been through anything?" I used to think. I didn't think so.

My other thoughts, along with many other men were, while you're matching jeopardy questions with your wife and kids, we're going through some real life drama. So what do you have for me that will be in my favor? Oh, I didn't think so.

This class taught us to walk away, and that women were always right. So in other words to stay out of jail young black men, let her act a fool and give her whatever she wants as long as you're with her. I had to put up with this crap for 26 weeks at $19.00 per class. Man nothing seemed to be in my favor.

"Mr. Stepney, if you want to stay out of jail, you need to realize you can't win, you need to leave your home and come back another day. You can't win in this world Mr. Stepney, you just have to live in it." This is what I was told one day by the counselor. This exhausted what little steam I had in my caboose.

"So what did you learn in class today Mr. Stepney?" my wife would ask. "Nothing that pertained to me or my situation." I would say. "Well I'm sure you can apply something to this household from your little class," she teased. "You sure don't need the police over here again, so you better say or do something," she threatened. I refused to live in fear, so one of us had to leave.

The teasing and threats went on so long I couldn't bear it anymore. I was in such a deep depression at times that I refused to show my face in public. Then it got so bad, I couldn't face the people at work. That was mainly because I could feel them talking about me and planning to get rid of me because things were falling apart in my life.

Through this period, I learned that a young black man is supposed to have it all together in the eyes of corporate America. If you don't, your livelihood is at risk at all times. If you're not smiling everyday, you have an attitude problem. "Boy we gave you a good job, so smile and be happy. What are you sad about? This is your life, let that other life go before we let you go!" Said the corporate mind.

"Mr. Stepney, it seems that you have a lot you're going through, but we need you here," The Human Resources Representative said. "So what are you saying?" I asked. "Mr. Stepney it's time you turn in your badge, your employment here is over." "What! I've given you five good years, several promotions, saved the company thousands of dollars, had all outstanding performance reviews, and you letting me go just like that!" I yelled. "Mr. Stepney, we didn't want to do it, but we had to," the representative dryly stated. "Okay then, I'm gone."

Corporate America stepped on my neck when I was down, and it hurt badly. I worked hard to get where I was, and I was very loyal. I guess my job was my second marriage that went bad. I knew then if I didn't do what they wanted when they wanted, our relationship was over. Just like my home marriage.

I went home to tell my wife what happened, and she asked me; "What time are you going job hunting?" This took me out of the shock I was in, and I knew she wasn't for me. Why this was happening to me, I wasn't sure, but something had to give before I gave myself or someone else a bullet.

I was broke down like and old Ford Escort, and I think that's what everyone wanted to see. I gave them what they wanted, and I hoped they were amused. I broke down and the breaking point had arrived. Now that I'm broke down, what you gonna do? I'll tell you what all of you are gonna do, you're gonna leave me the hell alone! Peace!

The Great Pretenders

This chapter goes out to a certain group of people. Parents who pretend to love their family, husbands and wives who pretend to love each other, corporate bosses who pretend to care about employees, ministers who pretend to be true messengers, presidents who pretend to be real leaders, whites who pretend to like blacks and other races, so called ballers who live with their mothers, women who pretend to have it going on, but are really on Section 8, business owners who pretend to be for the community, lawyers who pretend to be out for your best interest, friends who pretend to be your friend, and so on.

If this is you, you need to tighten up your program and just be real. What do you get out of being a pretender? Do you think a smart person is too narrow-minded to figure you out? Guess what, you've been figured out a long time ago, other people are just pretending like you!

To me, being a pretender is just wasted energy, sometime physical, mostly mental that you waste your time using just so you won't be figured out. Then what happens is you force others to pretend because they don't want to tell you about yourself.

In my life, I've experienced many ups and downs, ins and outs, and twists and turns. During these periods in my life, I found very few people were in my corner. No, I'm not mad just don't waste my time because eventually, I will cut the cord. Is this you? If it is, you know what I'm talking about.

Even though I didn't get to cut the cords of my own children, I cut the cords on a lot of so called friendships and other relationships. Even though cutting these cords left a bitter taste in my mouth, it took a lot of extra pressure off of my emotional being. That's what I want some pressure relief. It's like putting warm home cooked greens in a Tupperware container and when you put the lid on it swells. But when you crack that lid just a little, pressure is released.

I say that to say this, after I went from $19.63 an hour to $0.00 a week, everybody started acting funny. Why you acting funny? I'm not going to ask you for anything. Why you telling everybody else that I'm going down, but you coming over my house smiling in my face, checking my refrigerator?

Then there were the ones who wouldn't take my calls or anything, what the corporate demons don't want you to talk to me? Will you be any less of a person if we were still cool? No, you're just a pretender and you only want to be seen dealing with a certain kind of person. You would've been a good person if you just lent me an ear or a shoulder, you would've been real.

Why you asking other people how I'm doing when you know I called to talk to you? I'm still me, are you still you? Hell naw, what you wanna hear, I'm cracked out or something? I'm cool, it was just a job, and a job ain't nothing but work. Work for an hour, get paid for an hour, but never paid what you're worth. Don't play with me.

While everyone was judging me, including my wife, I decided to take a trip for a couple of weeks just to get away. But you know what? The same thing was with me, unhappiness and betrayal and it wouldn't leave me until I faced it head on. I felt like I was losing everything including my kids.

So I decided to come home after a long vacation to face the demons and try to start over again. I was running an emotional marathon and still had a long way to go until I crossed the finish line. The pretenders in my life had frustrated me, and I continued to let it eat away at me like acid. To cover these feelings, I started dating different women again to ease some of the pain inside. They very seldom made me happy, so I had different people to fulfill different needs. I knew this was a flaw that I had, and this flaw made me a pretender as well.

After a few months of living off of my savings, I thought I'd start job-hunting again. With my experience, it wouldn't be hard to land another decent gig, at least I thought. But I soon realized no matter how much experience you have the judgmental corporate demons don't want any gaps in your employment history. What they want is to steal you from another company, it seems sometime they don't want the hungry applicant they want the comfortable one.

After a lot of job hunting and little luck, I decided to do what I dreaded most. Go file for unemployment. My belief was and still is, if you're able to work, you need to work. But since the President had the world on lockdown, I had no choice. My plan was get some unemployment so I can at least eat and pay my child support. You know child support gonna get theirs, but I ain't mad as long as the kids eat.

By this time my wife looked at me as a failure and she moved back home with her parents. Even though I was a go-getter, I was still a failure to her. Fine, go be with your momma and daddy, you didn't have my back anyway. Not only that, if I'm not buying you anything, you have an attitude. Do you know anyone like that?

I really hated waiting on the mailman for my check, but at this point I didn't really have a choice. Even though I hated waiting on him, I was always happy to see him on Friday. You know what? When the work stops, the bills keep coming so I swallowed my pride and cashed them checks.

After I paid my bills each check, I usually had about $40.00 left to my name so I would get some groceries and a six-pack of beer. I used to always talk about my mother cutting out coupons, but I became the coupon king. And places I never used to shop became my favorite places, like Dollar General, Aldi, and Big Lots. Man $5.00 can keep your butt wiped and your skin smelling like fresh Ivory soap.

I kept plugging away because I always believed in good hard work. I landed some top-notch interviews, but since the job market was so tight, I was usually eliminated in the final round. To weed out so many applications, you had to be flawless in the process and I usually was, it was just when they went to do the background checks.

Some employers expressed their own personal opinion about my past, which had nothing to do with my work experience or what I could do for the company. One employer once told me, "Mr. Stepney, we were really impressed with your interview, experience, and test scores, but $46,000.00 is a little steep for a man with your background, this is just my opinion, but I'll give you a call if something else comes up." "Wow, thank you very much Mr. President" I said as I hung up.

After a while, I landed a couple of temporary jobs, but they weren't enough to cancel my check for. It seems that the temporary agencies always want to put a black man in the warehouse. "Mr. Stepney, you look very strong and in good condition, how would you like to fill 55 gallon drums and load them on a truck?" One placement coordinator asked me. "What about my supervisory skills and clerical abilities?" I asked. "Well, let's start you in the warehouse first," she added.

These actions and many more kept my confidence in a struggle, and it was so hard to find any balance within myself. I didn't have a Masters Degree in anything but everyday life, but everyday living, working, laughing, and crying gave me the experience and skill to work with and deal with anyone. After all, you needed on the job training anyway right?

Ring, ring, ring, "Hello," "Hi, is this Roooooomey?" "No, this is Rommey." "This is Sue from the agency, I wanted to know if you wanted to pass out cookies at the mall for 10 hours a day on Saturday and Sunday?" "Pass out cookies like chocolate chip?" I asked. "Yes, it pays $8.00 an hour," she added. "Would you have your man standing there passing out cookies?" "No, not ever." "Well give me the job you would give your man!" There was silence, I hung up the phone and cried.

For days I cried until it gave me a new strength, and it was time to really increase my efforts. It still seemed my so-called friends enjoyed what I was going through, and my wife enjoyed it even more. I tried to be strong for my kids because they need to see strength in their father. I wanted to accomplish so much for them, so they could see determination and inherit it.

I landed a small job as a dispatcher for a local agency in town dispatching drivers to pick employees on different temporary assignments. It was cool, but it was a dead end and I had to get off unemployment. I felt that money could be for someone who was disabled, I was ready and able.

Now that I was working, everyone wanted to come around and socialize, my wife even wanted to come home at one point. But my thought was, your love didn't make any sense, you're a pretender. While you all were pointing fingers at me, three were pointing back at you.

I plugged away at this job and developed a closer relationship with GOD. "Father I've been through so much, most of what I put myself through, but you never left my side. You loved me and saw fit when the world turned it's back on me. You kept me alive when I should've been gunned down. You protected my body when I took so many risks. Thank you, just as you never left my side, I will never leave yours, because without you, I am nothing." This is my prayer.

I started fine-tuning my mind, body, and spirit, and when I did that, I started becoming more at peace with myself. I had forgiven my parents of their shortcomings in life, those I hurt and betrayed, and those who hurt and betrayed me. I'm not perfect, but I recognized the areas in me that needed improvement, and as long as I take the proper steps, GOD will do the rest in time.

Once I did this, it was like I had taken my overall being to the cleaners and my eyes were opened to see things I never saw. I saw most of the world wasn't for my success or well-being, but now it didn't phase me because I was focused on my source, the stem, the head, GOD.

The few pretenders that were left in my life started to drift away as well, and it became so evident they wanted me to rot away. That was the only reason they were around because thy wanted to witness the destruction first hand. I wasn't mad though, I just let them fade away on their own, when I see you I'll speak, but it wasn't about spending any time. I learned that my life was messy when I was around messy people with messy minds.

Since I took work serious, I learned to channel my efforts into helping others as well. Sometimes I would cruise around just to see who could use some help. I didn't mind helping people who were honest about their situation, but I'm not giving you money for beer or smokes. The only thing I have for those people is advice. "Pull it together man," I would say.

My mind and heart continued to grow strong, and I kept on pushing. Ahhhhh push it, push it real good, remember that song by Salt-n-Peppa? As long as I kept pushing toward total self-improvement, I felt things would continue to get better. Keeping a steady relationship with the creator GOD, educating myself on a continuous basis, and keeping good company would keep negativity off my doorstep. No pretenders allowed!!

The Everyday Brother

Soon after I developed a greater confidence in GOD, my future, and myself I got a job offer from a company I interviewed with. It was for the low-income housing authority in the Columbus area. Columbus Metropolitan Housing Authority, or CMHA.

The position was for a custodian on the maintenance staff in the low-income apartments on the east and west sides of town. Even though I had went back to where I started, which was cleaning up after people, I looked at it as another chance to make things right with myself. I had no problems with working my way through the ranks, I done it before, and I could do it again.

The managers I interviewed with were two black men from the old school, Mr. Fredd and Mr. Vernon. They looked at my resume' and saw my strengths without judging me. They saw passion in my eyes and heard determination in my voice and overlooked my past. They thought about what I could do in the future.

I worked immediately under Mr. Fredd, and I showed my appreciation by working hard. He could've chosen any one of the candidates but he chose me, I owe part of my new start to him. I had a lot of ups and downs in my life, but he looked at my ups instead of my downs.

Being a custodian in the housing authority was very hard work, because it's almost like most of the people in the housing system don't care about themselves or how they live, so you almost have to care for them. But if you see them on the street scene they act like they've got it going on, but when you get to their house, it's like a junkyard. These people are pretenders.

The other pretenders in this world of low-income and section-8 housing are the young men who live off of the women. These are the brothers who save their little money and live with their girlfriends or baby's mommas who are only paying a small portion of rent. Sometimes that's anywhere from $0.00 to $100.00, and then you're late paying that.

My question is this, why are you sitting there with Jordan's on and a $100.00 jersey on playing play station while the apartment is in filth and your baby has no food? Why is the young woman sporting Louis V bags, Baby Phat, and Apple Bottom Jeans and your children don't have a bed to sleep in? You're selfish, and have no clue about life. You're a pretender!

Why is it that you have the ability to work, but only settle for what the system will give you and then complain about not having anything? Why is it you have an attitude from the first of the month to the tenth, then the rest of the month you're crying the system don't care about you? Is it because you spent your check on Grey Goose, new shoes and a hairdo? Now you're mad because you didn't budget your food stamp card and brought ribs and shrimp for a party in your small apartment and now there's nothing left? Who you mad at, aren't you the pretender?

Cleaning up and fixing things for this selfish group only increased my vision. But I do give props to the ones who need this assistance and keep their places clean. Those are the elderly, the disabled, mothers and fathers who are in school working part-time to support their children, and people with mental issues.

But enough of calling people out, because I still had some upcoming issues that I needed to handle. I was still working hard in this world and giving people loving advice at the same time. I wanted to see people free of making bad decisions and just settling for anything. I wanted to help people free themselves of hatred toward one another by showing them love. I wanted happiness for everyone.

One day while I was so happy-go-lucky, I received my paycheck, and when I opened it my smile turned into a frown. I had worked 80 long hard hours and my check was $98.00! What in the hell happened?

The Everyday Brother

I checked the column with all of my deductions, and every thing was cool all the way from retirement to union dues. Wait a minute, child/spousal support? Where did the spousal come in?

Here they were again, child support robbing me blind and not caring an ounce about a hard-working man with a vision who already loves and cares for his kids. "Hello, is this my child support officer my name is Rommey, here's my social security number," I said. "Let me pull you up on the screen," she said with a prejudiced voice. "Oh yes, it seems you have a court order to pay that amount for your daughter," she said. "Why didn't I get some kind of notice for a hearing or something?" I asked.

The insensitive support officer told me to go to the courthouse to get copies of the documents. I did so, and apparently my wife at the time filed for a divorce, lied about my income, and intentionally had the papers sent to a Rebuilding Lives apartment complex. This rebuilding lives complex housed ex-cons, ex-drug users, and homeless people trying to rebuild their lives. This was like a smack in the face with a plan to destroy me. Once again this is where she wanted to see me.

Since I never received the papers, it looked to the court like I didn't care about my daughter or anything. So the court accepted anything she said without investigating why I didn't receive the paperwork. You get no chances with Franklin County as a black man it's straight to the sewer.

I did everything I could to plead my case, and I even told them how I couldn't live off of $98.00 every two weeks and how she lied to the court. As I talked to the clerk with tears running down my face, he simply said, "Well the best thing to do is get an attorney." "I don't know any for $98.00, I want to take care of my children I'm a good loving father, I just need to live too!" I shouted with a mouth full of tears.

It seemed that the clerk I was talking to, was enjoying my pain and suffering. He was a young tall white man who had the squint in his eyes of disgust and the smirk on his face like the smirk I grew up hating. "Sir, you heard what I said, have a good day," he said with a devilish smile. I had to make a call.

"Hey, why would you do something like that? Why would you lie about my income and have my paperwork sent to that place?" I asked. "First of all, don't call me on my job, second, I thought you would be there since you're trying to get your life together," she said. "You know where I live, you've rode by there so many times!" I shouted. "Yell at me again, and I'll call the State Trooper and tell them you threatened to kill me, you know this is a state building," she said. I hung up.

I didn't mind the divorce, because I wanted one myself, I just didn't have the money at the time. But what I figured is this. A woman can sometimes see the potential in a struggling man before he can, but if she knows he's a good man trying hard, she will put the system on him. Because her thought is, I can't stop him, but I can slow him down by putting the system on him. So without me black man, you will suffer. That's the thought of a simple, selfish woman.

So I called an attorney, one I heard on the radio many times. She was a black attorney who sounded like she could be of some help according to her advertisement. When I go to the office, she tells me what it would cost to have everything reversed, the retainer was well over a thousand dollars, and money I didn't have.

After I was blessed with the help of someone dear to me, I took care of my business to get the paperwork filed. Once I paid the money, it took a week to get the paperwork filed, and why did it take so long? Hell, I don't know. This lawyer took my money and things went at a snails pace. All I could think about was how many more $98.00 checks I would receive.

After the paperwork was filed, I met with the attorney again to see when I could get a court date. "Mr. Stepney, it will be a couple of months before you get a court date," she said. "So you're saying I have to live off of $98.00 for the next couple of months?" I asked. "I hate to say this, but you're just going to have to tuff it out," she said with a smirk to say sorry about your luck I got your money now, better you than me.

As evil thoughts took over my flesh, all I could feel was hatred toward anyone who tried to keep me in the battle between good and evil. The devil had clouded my mind with visions of hatred and torture, and nothing could kill these visions but hard prayer and faith. So I began to kill these visions with words of prayer that I alone could not muster up.

The next couple of months were hard, but I kept easy and prayerful and tried not to think of the amount of money I was receiving at the end of each pay period. Can you imagine cleaning up after people, making repairs, picking up trash, and cleaning nasty stoves and refrigerators for $98.00 every two weeks? It would drive you crazy if you focused on it. I kept positive and kept my pocket bible to keep my sanity.

During this period, I had been doing some research on business and home-based businesses. I wanted a good business of my own where I would be rewarded for my efforts, not just get an hourly wage and one raise a year. Financially it wasn't healthy to work until exhaustion only to get what someone feels you should earn by the hour.

"Heavenly father, I've been through so much in my years in this physical body. I've been in physical and emotional sin the majority of my days and I ask again your forgiveness. I've been looking for love through the wrong people in the wrong places only to find hurt and disappointment. I've had faith in people who didn't believe in me, and I've had financial ups and downs. GOD, place me in a position where I can continue to improve myself and help others. I'm not looking to get rich overnight, but I just want what you have for me. This is my prayer, amen."

I continued to work hard for my $98.00 every two weeks, letting the bills pile up and forcing a smile all at same time. But I had a feeling in me that everything would be okay and I knew it was because I really released everything to GOD this time. I quit struggling with myself and learned to give every spell that someone cast on me to GOD so he can put in his book for him to handle in his time.

A few weeks later, I got a call from my good friend Dr. Rupert Bushner Jr., an Adventist minister out of Florida who grew up in Akron, Ohio.

"Hey Rome, Rome, what's up man?" Trying to make it, giving it all to the creator," I said. "Man, I got something for you that's going to change your life!" He said. It's changed so many lives and it's changed mine too!" He added happily. "Well send me some info," I said. "Cool, I'm putting it in the mail today, call me when you get it," he said. "Will do my brother, peace!"

I received the packet of information, and it was about a company called Usana, which means true health in the Greek-Latin language. Usana has a broad range of products to improve your health, from natural skin care to vitamins and minerals, to meal replacement shakes and nutrition bars. And it gave specific breakdown of its manufacturing practices and research, which showed the numbers and many other interesting facts.

The other interesting thing about these products was they were not in stores for sale. The founder, Dr. Myron Wentz has it set up through the distribution of home-based business owners through the power of network marketing. I had to ask myself, what is network marketing? So I did my research on marketing and network marketing distributors.

In my research, I found that network marketing is the way to create wealth. Not only that, I would be helping myself and others improve their lives. And on top of that, I would get paid to keep myself healthy!

Also in my research, I found that Usana was ranked #9 in Business Weeks top 100 small companies, and #16 in Forbes top 200 companies. And since then, has climbed to #3 in Business Week and #5 in Forbes. With these numbers, I felt I could use a boost in my income because the $98.00 checks were killing me, so I became a home-based business owner.

I started my business introducing the products and opportunity to friends and relatives. It was a shame how so many people that claimed they were close to me showed no support. Even though I had quality products of my own, they still chose to go to the health store. They were still pretenders.

My business took a slow start, but it was steady, and the good thing about it was I was helping others take a turn in their lives to better health. This increased my focus on self-improvement, and gave me a greater sense of accomplishment.

Time flew and my court date had arrived to see if I could get this mess settled. I told my attorney how unfair I was treated and it should be mentioned to the court how this woman lied just so I could suffer more. "That's not even the issue," she said. "Well I'll tell the judge myself," I said. "Mr. Stepney, the judge doesn't want to hear you, that's what you paid me for," she said. I've heard that before.

Well, she was right. And what did I pay you for? I had to ask myself. She talked more to my ex-wife than she did to me. Okay, you got my money, but I should've done the math. 1 single black female attorney + an office full of single black females + 1 bitter ex-wife + 1 female judge = nothing happening for me.

In the courtroom, the female judge spoke with a smile to the women, and never looked my way. She unhappily made an adjustment that was unfair in the first place. Never acknowledging the dishonesty, she said to her, "simple mistake." I knew the pretenders had me outnumbered for the moment, but I just decided to do me and they could do themselves.

I say that to say this, so many people put so much time in going to school for an income, not to truly make a difference in peoples' lives. Do you spend years in college for the dollars or to be true to someone? Do you stand for what's right, or do stand to sit in the Benz or BMW at the end of the day?

I once heard someone say, helping others and being true to him or her is like paying rent to get to heaven. These bodies and minds are on a lease, when we turn them in there should be no damage or it will cost us. We damage these minds and bodies by hating each other, falsely accusing, and selfishly doing things to hurt others for our own gain. We show no support when support is much needed. We show no love because we don't truly love ourselves.

Until we change our ways, we will continue to be pretenders in every way. Until we are true to ourselves, we can't be true to anyone else no matter what you do. What is untrue? It's make believe, it's a lie or pretend. And as long as you're a pretender, you are the weakest link! Goodbye!

The Quest For Love

The quest for love is something that I've always made harder than what it really was. I used to spend time looking for that right person to love me, that right group of friends, and so on. But in my opinion, when we develop a relationship with GOD, love and appreciate his wonderful creations, he puts love in our hearts.

Without love there is hatred, fear, envy, jealousy, selfishness, and so many other feelings that we adopt in our lives that make us so incomplete. We have recycled so many acts of hatred through the years, and it really sounds simple to hate someone or judge them just because people did it years ago.

To me, love starts at home and is duplicated throughout. Whatever we give our children, family and friends in most cases; they will give to someone else. We put ourselves at a dead end when love has an imbalance. If I have love for you, but you don't have love for me, love is not duplicated and it goes nowhere.

We allow hateful, violent, and sex ridden videos and games to enter our households. Then when there is a crime on the street, some of us are wondering what happened. We have reality shows where there's so much competition that breeds hate and dislike. Man against woman, black vs. white, nation against nation and so on.

When there is the love of GOD in you, there is a need and desire to want the best for our children. Men and women love each other and team up to want the best for our kids. Without true love, we make so many poor choices that require recovery time which take so much out of us and away from us.

Why are we watching shows on TV where a nanny has to come in and get our bad children together? True love should bring an automatic discipline in our lives to handle our children on our own. Why are we putting our babies in dumpsters, scalding them, throwing them in rivers and blowing their brains out? We need love.

Why are there thirty-year-old men walking down the street with their pants down to their knees having visions of murder? Better yet, why are there thirty-year-old men talking about the latest rap videos and who is about to blast who?

Why do so many white Americans love Michael Jordan, Tiger woods, and Lebron James, but hate the average black man on the street? Why do you choose whom to love? True love is automatic and is meant for everyone.

Why are there so many grandmothers under forty who deny their grandchildren? Why are there so many children who disrespect their parents? Where is the love? Love shouldn't stop at one person. It should go through one person touching another person.

I learned in my life when I developed a true love for our creator, his love was already in me. No more bitterness, anger, fear, or anything else. I have forgiven myself, and others. It's possible for you to do it too.

True love also put it in my heart to open my home to my stepfather when he needed a place to live. The love of GOD also allowed my biological father to give his life to Christ, he is now a leader of his church and doing several acts of kindness for the community. True love allowed me to accept my mother and many others for who they are, and what they believe in.

No one should be homeless, poor, or alone, no one should feel emptiness or hate. One Adam and one Eve. Before the flood, only Noah and his family were on the ark. Where did we all come from? Don't strain your brain, I'll ask you a simple one. Can a black man give a white man blood or a kidney?

Let's get off of ourselves and make it about someone else. Not just for a day, but forever. One GOD, One Blood, One Love. I love you, peace.

    Rommey.

About the Author

I have wanted to write this particular book for some time now. The purpose of my book is to reach out to many young people and parents who are looking for a solution to the everyday pressures of life. It is my desire to be able to help anyone who crosses my path. While I am waiting for my book to be released, I am also perusing my desire to open a youth center for young people from all walks of life. In my dealings with young people, I've learned that there is a need to provide for the interaction of children being raised in the inner city with children being raised in the suburbs. Young people can learn from one another, and so can adults.